Royal-ish

First published in 2024 by HarperCollins *Children's Books*
An imprint of HarperCollins *Publishers* India
4th Floor, Tower A, Building No. 10, DLF Cyber City,
DLF Phase II, Gurugram, Haryana – 122002

2 4 6 8 10 9 7 5 3 1

P-ISBN: 978-93-6213-686-2
E-ISBN: 978-93-6213-699-2

Cover design and art by Lee-Roy Lahey
Inside illustrations by Lee-Roy Lahey

Typeset in 12/16.2 Adobe Garamond at
HarperCollins *Publishers* India

Printed and bound at Thomson Press India Ltd

MIX
Paper | Supporting responsible forestry
FSC® C010615

This book is produced from independently certified FSC® paper
to ensure responsible forest management.

Royal-ish

Lily's Adventures in Bagradoo

Amrita Gandhi

Illustrated by Lee-Roy Lahey

HARPERCOLLINS
CHILDREN'S BOOKS

'This book has a bit of everything—lavish palaces, eccentric royals, a ledger of boons, a robot jester, mythical flora and fauna and a lot of adventure!
Go royal and royal-ish as you travel to the exotic Bagradoo with Amrita Gandhi's unputdownable book.'

Ruskin Bond
bestselling children's author

'*Royal-ish* is a rollicking tale about an awkward teen with an oversized backpack who sets out to find her roots in mystical Bagradoo Island, that has urgent conservation issues which Lily helps to resolve.
The story unfolds through witty dialogue and wonderfully whacky events like a fashion contest between a crocodile and a princess!
Easy to read, hard to put down.'

Zai Whitaker
author and naturalist

Contents

Prologue

Meet Lily Ray of Puddleton. Seventh grader, nature vlogger and owner of more pairs of gumboots than most people own socks. Lily was Puddleton Middle School's greatest wildlife enthusiast.

Unfortunately for Lily, "wildlife" in the small, rainy suburb of Puddleton consisted of a pair of dragonflies, one snail and—

on a very exciting day—a frog spotted at the community pond, of which Lily knew every slushy corner.

Lily's love for sloshing about in one of her many gumboots, exploring the wonders of Puddleton pond, did not make her the most popular girl at school. In fact, the school's in-crowd, led by the popular Sasha Smith, had some special nicknames for Lily—puddle pusher, marsh hopper and even Her Royal Slime-ness.

'Shake it off, like water off a duck's back,' her mother told her, trying to be helpful.

'Thanks Mom, and now I'm a duck?'

'No Lily, you're a budding scientist. Be proud of who you are.'

Lily tried her best to brush these comments aside.

With scientist parents who worked all day, the pond was how Lily kept busy. So she took her mother's advice and dug her heels in. She started a vlog about what she knew best—the wildlife of Puddleton pond. She affectionately called her vlog the "Glog"—G for Gumboots. Surprise, surprise, the Glog was not popular with the kids at school, for whom Sasha's high-street shoe vlog was all the rage. But Lily got better at it each day. After all, it was while vlogging—or should we say, "Glogging"—that she could be herself and truly shine. Little did Lily know that her Glog would one day turn her humdrum days into the adventure of a lifetime.

KEEP CALM AND CARRY ON GLOGGING

Hi friends, I'm Lily Ray, a seventh grader, nature vlogger and gumboot enthusiast.

If you love a wet wade in a marsh, a damp squelch in a swamp, a picnic by a puddle, with a net in hand and gumboots on your feet, then the Glog is the vlog for you.

To those of you tuning in for the first time, I'd like to extend my hearty marsh-hellos.

And those of you who stumbled upon the Glog while searching for my classmate Sasha's shoe vlog, the Shlog, let me redirect you.

But before you go, I'd like to say that the Glog may not be glam, but our following is loyal, and we try to give you enough local scoop about swamp life to make you want to stick around. *Stick* around, get it?

You're still here? Great, let's wade right in!

As promised, let me give you a sneak peek into the latest additions to my gumboot collection.

Trust me, you need a pair for every type of swamp.

Meet my maroon Moon Landers—these boots have soles so thick that they make strolling through tarry peat bogs feel like a walk in the park.

Next come my classy Knee Highs. They sound trendy, but let me tell you, they are more than that. Knee Highs are the perfect accessory for pond wading, though the truth is that nothing can prevent a tadpole from getting between your toes.

And now, fellow Gloggers, it's time to meet the newest member of my gumboot collection.

Introducing … the … Five Toe Squelchers!

Here they are, everyone. They may not be runway-ready, but they give you that unshakable grip when you need to crouch in a pool of sludge to photograph a frog that refuses to sit still!

Get your own pair of Five Toe Squelchers or, better yet, borrow one! We are all about squelching lightly on our planet.

Oh! I just received a puke emoji from Sasha's Shlog—never thought they'd even notice me. I take it as a badge of honour, and who knows, these Squelchers might just be in fashion one day …

But that's not all folks—I have some breaking news for you!

As you may know, I've been a bit quiet on the marsh front since the discovery of the Blue Crowned frog.

For those of you who missed that big discovery—here's a picture of me with the rare Blue Crowned frog I found right here at Puddleton pond, the frog that scientists had all but given up on as extinct.

The zoological society was so excited at my discovery that they named the frog after me.

With the naming of *Regium Lily Anura,* I got a new name too.

One that, shall we say, really stuck.

Literally.

"Her Royal Slime-ness of Puddleton," it said on a paper crown stuck on my school locker.

Witty. But I kept calm and carried on Glogging until one day something totally unexpected happened.

I was messing around in my mom's lab when …

Mom's lab? Yes, my parents are scientists, specifically geneticists who're working on building a robot that studies genes. Safe to say, they spend a lot of time in the lab and, as a result, I spend a lot of *my* time after school in the lab, waiting while they "wrap up work" that they just seem to get more and more wrapped up in.

I pretty much grew up in the lab … Just look at these pictures of me as a baby.

Yes, the lab coat onesie is photoshopped, but you get the drift.

Anyway, the other day, I was tinkering with some beakers and test tubes. A little rub here, a drop there, zip and zap—and before you know it, I was testing my DNA in the algorithm wizard robot my mom was building. I scanned the results to discover that I share a teeny tiny amount of genetic material with … you won't believe this … this calls for a drum roll … the royal family of the island kingdom of Bagradoo!

'Bagra-whoooooo?' My question exactly. Apparently, it is the royal family of Bagradoo.

I can practically hear Sasha's friends in middle school say:

That Lily Ray—related to royalty?

Lily Ray, who spends recess plogging near the pond …

And stays back for extra geography credits 😆🤮

She's from an island kingdom? 🤦‍♀️😮👑

Well, keep your boots on everyone, I am not royal enough to lay stake to a share of the kingdom. Just distantly related enough to say hello, how do you do, or however it is one greets royals these days. But I was not going to let this chance slip, because here's what happened next.

I decided to do a quick search on Bagradoo and discovered that this is no mere kingdom with palaces, jewels and carriages.

This island kingdom is home to the most amazing and rare species of plant and animal life that don't exist anywhere else in the world. Safe to say, there's more to my Glog than stuff about Puddleton pond.

So, I decided to take things into my own letter-writing hand and wrote to King Khair, the King of Bagradoo. I introduced myself as a nature vlogger and sent him pictures of my finds at Puddleton, including a "Snailfee" from our local marsh. He wrote back—yes, people, the King wrote back. To little old me. I have it right here, letter head and all—saying he was a photographer too and sent me pictures of the palace's "little flower patch", which is Royal lingo for a spectacular conservatory of flowers complete with rare butterflies and singing frogs. You've got to hand it to royalty for doing things with style because he then … *wait for it* … enclosed cruise ship tickets for me to make an officiallllll voyyyyyaggge to visit the royal family of Bagradoo!!!

So, Lily asked her parents if she could go.

Naturally, they were a bit sceptical at first about sending her to a faraway kingdom on a holiday to visit "relatives" she didn't know. But with a good dose of reasoning, pleading and guilt-tripping about the long summers she had spent in the lab every year, Lily got her parents to say yes.

They agreed to let her go on one condition. Being the robot scientists they were, they built Lily her very own pocket-sized robotic diary. They called it Al the Pal.

'I know I don't have too many friends, Mom, but you really didn't need to build me one,' Lily said with a smile.

'It's just a little gadget for your trip, darling. You can vlog with it, plan your schedule, write a diary and call us. It even has a funny joke button if you're bored or homesick.'

I am to carry this little pocket diary wherever I go. My very own digital diary, planner, rare species scanner, camera and scheduler rolled into one.

And right now, fellow Gloggers, I am coming to you live from my cruise ship cabin.

Yes, you heard right—my cruise ship cabbbbinn!

I am just beginning to glimpse the island of Bagradoo in the distance …

Lily's phone rang, bringing the Glog to a sudden stop. It was her mother, Rita, speaking to her from the lab.

'Sorry friends, this is Mom calling. I have to take this.'

At the other end of the phone, Dr Rita Ray could be heard speaking in a calm voice with a slight hint of motherly worry.

'Hi, Lilykins. Are you nearly there yet?'

'Hi Mom, yes, nearly there—and I think I can see the isssssssssland …'

'This is your big adventure, sweetie. But remember, be careful, and only get into the car sent by the palace, okay? You should see a sign with your name on it as soon as you step off the ship.'

'Okay Mom, I won't talk to strangers, yada yada … which means I won't talk to anybody at all,' Lily replied, trying her best to not sound nervous.

'Very funny, Lily. You know what I mean. Call me every day, okay?'

'Of course, Mom. And if I need to talk to you and there's no connection, there's always Al the Pal, right?'

'Yes sweetie. Al's your Pal. Just press the "Mom" button!' They both laughed.

'Okay Mom—got to go now, okay? I've got to look out for that sign from the palace,' said Lily.

Lily couldn't believe she had said the word "palace". She did a little cartwheel, covering every inch of her tiny cabin. Then, she regained her composure and put on her gear. Her heavy backpack, crammed with stuff for any tropical eventuality, teetered over her head and made her wobble a bit. She wondered if she should have listened to her mom and packed fewer gumboots. She hooked on a second bag in the front, the one with Al the Pal in it, and carefully bent over to pick up her selfie stick in one hand and a water bottle in the other. Lily then stepped out onto the cruise deck, looking every bit the tourist she was, with a smile bright enough to illuminate a small kingdom.

1

Embarrassing Entrance

A magical scene greeted Lily at the port of Bagradoo.

The warm afternoon light made patterns on the sea water, making it look like it was dancing. The lagoon all around her was a patchwork of blues. Little waves of turquoise, teal, azure, cobalt and more shades of blue than she could name bobbed up and down like blue jelly. In the distance lay powdery soft white sand and, just beyond the shore, a port buzzing with life. Lily breathed in the smell of the sun and the sea, the fragrance of flowers and fruit and something strangely familiar … the scent of waffles!

'I smell waffles,' said Lily into her camera as she recorded her arrival video.

'The aroma of fresh waffles is from a fruit tree that grows only in Bagradoo,' a peculiar robotic voice piped in from her front pack. 'The Waffalagooz is a tropical tree with round juicy white fruits and yellow flowers, whose scent reminds one of Belgian waffles.'

'Uuh, thanks?' said Lily slowly, unsure of how to interact with a speaking non-person.

'You're welcome. Oh, and welcome to Bagradoo.'

Tourists in summer hats beamed in wide-eyed excitement, many already wondering where the waffle shop was. And then, Lily noticed the locals, for whom this island was home. 'Imagine living in Bagradoo!' She sighed. Everywhere people looked busy—buying and selling things, talking, laughing, even arguing—with a mix of big city energy and holiday island vibes.

Outdoor shops with white wicker awnings sold silk scarves and chic hats. In the distance, sports cars and canopied bicycle taxis shared the street with little yellow buses whose conductors were dressed in floral shirts. But what set this view apart from anything Lily had ever imagined were the delicate creepers and vines bursting with fruit and flowers. They wrapped themselves around buildings, lampposts, balconies and traffic lights. The vines were studded with delicate flowers and fruit that smelled like candy, with butterflies and birds flitting in and out of them. Lily felt like she had arrived in a giant conservatory where the domed glass ceiling was the blue sky itself. She loved her home, but if any place could be the opposite of Puddleton, Bagradoo was it. Yet, for some strange reason, Lily felt she'd come home.

'Miss Lily, it's time to get you to your car,' said a cruise attendant. 'We must look out for the sign with your name on it from …' He consulted the clipboard he was holding. 'From the Bagradoo Palace? Impressive,' he added with a smile.

Lily smiled back. 'Yes, I've been asked to look out for a sign with my name.'

'Sign with my name on it, sign with my name on it,' Lily repeated to herself as she scanned a dozen name cards of people waiting to be received at the port.

A group of dancers sashayed by, writing the name "Lily" in the air with swirling ribbons. Unknown to Lily, this grand display was her welcome party. Likewise, the palace party did not expect the royal family's guest to be an awkward tween with an oversized backpack.

Lily found herself in the midst of their elaborate twirling dance, and when she emerged, she had lost sight of the cruise attendant. However, something interesting caught her eye—a winding path of tiny antique shops selling things she had never seen, not even on the best day at the local flea market in Puddleton. Lily made her way to the shops. As she browsed some antique bric-à-brac—dusty paintings, china, lampshades, dressers and mirrors—a little boy in a school uniform came forward to help her. To her surprise, he spoke with a distinct Australian accent.

'Hello Miss, welcome to my uncle's antique store. Would you like to try this incense? It's got a great eucalyptus aroma that will take you right back to Australia if you're homesick.' Then he paused and added, 'What do you think? I'm practising my sales pitch to tourists. For when I grow up, you know.'

'Thanks, I'm just browsing,' replied Lily, with a laugh. 'And I'm English.'

The boy immediately switched to the Queen's English. 'In that case, could I interest you in this vintage tea set, Miss? Great for a pot of Darjeeling, or are you more of an Earl Grey person?'

Lily laughed. 'Good accent.'

Just then, a curious little dusty and somewhat dented half-moon shaped pearl caught her eye. It was resting on a velvet cushion right next to the teapot. She touched it gently, but before she could pick it up, the shop owner whisked it away.

'This one is not for sale,' he muttered, somewhat gruffly.

'Sure, no problem,' said Lily. 'I was just looking.'

'Scheduled to be in the palace car; scheduled to be in the palace car,' said a voice from her front backpack.

'Yes, Al, I know, but I couldn't find the sign with my name on it.'

'Proceed to plan B,' said Al. 'Though what that is, I don't know.'

'That's helpful, thanks Al,' said Lily. 'I saw lots of signs for taxis. Let's get one.'

'Finally,' said Al.

'Can you take me to the Bagradoo Palace?' Lily asked a kind-looking cab driver whose car had a bright floral canopy, magazines and piped music.

'Sure I can. Nice address,' the driver replied with a smile.

'Thanks,' said Lily.

As the car rumbled to a start, Lily felt a tap on her elbow. She immediately recognized the kid from the store. 'It's yours for a tenner,' he said, handing her the little half-moon pearl she had all but forgotten.

'But it wasn't on sale,' Lily reminded him.

'It is now, if you want it,' said the boy. 'No pressure, but uncle said you could have it—since business has been slow today.'

Before she could say anything more, Lily found herself in possession of the pearl that she wasn't sure she wanted.

The taxi quickly swerved away, and soon the bustling, friendly bazaar gave way to sweeping fort walls, gradually leading to an imposing palace. The Bagradoo Palace was meant to make its visitor's jaw drop. For one, you had to really lift your head up high to get a full look. And what you saw was nothing short of majestic.

Lily looked up and gulped. If the palace looked intimidating from afar, it was overwhelming up close. It resembled a grand sculpture in itself—an artist's creation of pillars, arches, carvings, glass and domes. Intertwined with these structures were Bagradoo's vines, but here they were pruned to perfection. Flowering climbers cascaded down from balconies in ornamental shapes. Below, tiered gardens dotted with artfully shaped fruit trees and sculptures made the place look like it belonged in a fairytale. All of this unfolded against the backdrop of towering mountains with tumbling waterfalls.

'Al, you there?'

'Oh yes, I'm here alright. I was just thinking of taking a nap … the summer air, you know … so soothing …'

'Okay, Al, but have you seen the palace?'

'Umm no, but I can see that protein bar wrapper you shoved into the backpack. Could have been worse, I suppose. Could have been a banana peel.'

'Al, this palace is huge. It is grand. I'm not sure I can do this; it's too overwhelming for little old me from Puddleton. I mean, why would they want to meet me? What am I doing here?'

'Well, a bit late for all of that, don't you think? But let me check … oh yes, to answer your question about what you are doing here. You are sitting in a somewhat bumpy ride, en route to the historic Bagradoo Palace.'

'I know, I know, Al … I just wish I had at the very least packed those linen trousers Mom told me to take … I mean, I want to make a good first impression. Well, maybe they'll all be busy taking their royal naps and giving orders or whatever royals do, and won't see me when I come in, and I can just sneak into my room and change into those jeans I packed …'

'Jeans. Hmm. Elegant.'

'Funny, Al,' said Lily, pulling out her camera and selfie stick.

`Here we are folks, this is so exciting! I am at Bagradoo Palace. Check this outttt.`

Lily's smile was bigger than usual, her tone three times as chipper.

'No one's buying the tone,' said Al from the backpack. 'One more take?'

'Seriously?' said Lily. 'You're giving me tips on my Glog now, Al?'

'Just saying you sounded a bit forced.'

'Okay, if you say so, Al. I mean, what do I know … I'm just a real person, right?' said Lily.

'That hurt my non-feelings,' said Al.

This made Lily laugh. She tried another take.

`So here I am, folks, and so very nervous, to tell you the truth. I've been excited all along, but now, seeing this amazing palace, I must say, I am kind of intimidated. I wish I'd listened to Mom and brought those linen pants after all.`

'Much better,' said Al. 'See, you've got six new likes.'

'Very funny again, Al,' said Lily, already feeling a bit more like herself.

She was just about done with her vlog when the cab sputtered to a stop, not quite able to make the sharpest of the curves leading up to the palace.

Of all the places where one would not want one's ride to break down, this would be at the top, but break down it did.

Palace guards helped push the car up the last curve. Lily got down, paid the driver with the island bills that her mother had sent with her, put on her towering backpack and clutched the smaller one with Al in front of her. Straightening herself, she walked up the steps, trying to look as much the royal guest as her creased clothes, oversized baggage and sneakers would allow.

As she was ushered into a grand glass ballroom, Lily's jaw dropped a bit more. Sunlight streamed in through stained-glass windows, creating a kaleidoscope of light around the room. Huge portraits of the royal family hung on invisible strings. Giant flowers in dramatic arrangements filled the room with a cool fragrance. Lounge chairs, elegantly placed, looked terribly comfortable but too beautiful for her to sit on. A few ridiculously colourful butterflies flitted in and out of the windows.

'It's not every day that you're speechless,' said Al. 'The palace must really be something.'

'Uh-huh,' whispered Lily as she was led past the grand ballroom into an adjacent room that, though cosier, was no less impressive, with a high ceiling, silk sofas and cushions and what could only be members of the royal family sitting around. Lily gulped.

'Welcome, welcome, my dear. It looks like the welcome party missed you completely.'

The booming voice belonged to King Khair, the King of Bagradoo himself. As he got up from his armchair, dressed casually in a Hawaiian shirt, there was no mistaking he was King alright, what with his strong voice and perfectly coiffed beard.

'Pashmina, meet Lily, a nature photographer from England who is here to learn more about Bagradoo's nature, and to tell us a bit about it too,' said King Khair to his daughter.

Princess Pashmina looked up from her lounging position on a chaise, flipping the pages of a fashion magazine with her own picture on the cover. She flashed a little smile but then glanced in mild horror at Lily's teetering backpack.

'Oh, hi,' said Princess Pashmina. 'I don't suppose you have anything in there for tonight's party?'

'Oh, uhm,' stammered Lily, at this point really wishing she had brought those linen pants. But as Lily lowered her backpack, what her mother had warned her would happen, happened.

With a thud, the overstuffed rucksack landed on the floor and flew open. A jumbo roll of toilet paper sprang out, bounced on the gleaming floor, did a hop and a skip and, as if in slow motion, unravelled and sent itself streaming down a set of grand stairs, cascading down like a white carpet.

'Ah, so it looks like we're hosting a white carpet gala tonight. I always thought red carpets were so overdone,' said a cheeky voice, clearly enjoying his own sense of humour. It was the last family member in the room Lily was yet to speak to. 'Oh, or are we camping instead?' he asked, looking at the portable solar kettle that had burst out of Lily's bag. 'Since you seem all set for the great outdoors, I hope you've packed a torch and a tent,' the boy added with a chuckle as Lily blushed, totally mortified.

'Oh, come, come, DJ,' said the King with a good-hearted chuckle. 'Lily just wasn't sure if she would get the supplies she needed in a faraway kingdom like ours. Lily, meet DJ, my nephew. He has a sense of humour that keeps us all in good cheer. DJ, Pashmina, please help Lily feel at home, would you?'

'Well, yes, of course,' said DJ. 'But while you've clearly packed everything but the kitchen sink, we really do hope you have something silver or white for tonight's party.'

At this point, Lily didn't know what to say.

'Don't worry, Lily, we'll get you sorted,' said the Princess. She tapped lightly on her phone. 'My style team will find something for you in just a bit.'

'Show Lily to her room,' said King Khair to a person-in-waiting who, having cleared the toilet roll, was now helping Lily with her luggage, eager to whisk the unseemly mess from the palace living room.

When they had turned the corner, away from the family, Lily muttered to herself, 'What was I thinking, packing household supplies to stay in a palace?'

'I was going to say, a bit overboard with the toilet paper, huh?' said Al. 'As first impressions go, would you like to rate yourself on a scale of 1–5? Consider this a learning exercise.'

'Thanks, but no, Al,' said Lily, trying her best not to think about the grand embarrassment that was her entrance.

'Follow me, please. This way to your room, Miss,' said the attendant, this time relieving her of the bag with Al the Pal in it too.

On the way to Lily's room, there was plenty to distract her. Every turn was an opportunity for a photograph, but Lily was too in awe to even reach for her camera. They passed courtyards with marble structures and water fountains glittering in the afternoon light. Giant moss-covered urns stood in shady corners, and dotting the way were small ponds with pink miniature water lilies. A blue- and gold-winged butterfly landed on Lily's nose and then flitted away, as if beckoning Lily to follow. The palace attendant was long out of sight anyway, so Lily followed the colourful creature before it vanished again.

She was indoors once again with no idea which way to turn, when she found herself standing in front of a room whose door was ajar. The cool air and fragrance wafting out of the room made Lily want to walk in. It smelled of books, always a favourite for Lily. There was no turning back for her now.

Lily ventured in silently. Wooden shelves stacked with old leather-bound volumes lined the walls floor-to-ceiling, and dog-eared parchment papers with detailed diagrams and ink drawings, maps and botanical drawings of rare-looking plants were spread across the tables and shelves all around. She then saw a big wooden desk with bubbling beakers and an old microscope.

'You do need to knock before you come in here to my den, young lady,' said a kind voice. Lily had not noticed an old gentleman at work behind a tall pile of parchment papers on the desk.

'I'm sorry. It's just that I kind of adore books and ... plant species ...' said Lily awkwardly.

'Then you'll see plenty to keep you busy in Bagradoo. You can expect a few surprises,' he said with a chuckle. 'But next time, be sure to knock. No one comes in here without my permission.'

An announcement interrupted them from the speakers overhead. 'Paging Miss Lily Ray for her makeover.'

'Got to go, I think. Sorry I walked in like that. Nice to meet you, Sir.'

'Nice to meet you too, Lily, you can call me Quill.'

'Paging Miss Lily for her makeover, paging Miss Lily for her makeover,' the overhead announcement continued, getting louder each time. Lily hurried out.

'Oh, there you are, Miss,' said the palace attendant, who at some point had realized that Lily wasn't following him. 'Let me escort you to the fashion studio.'

Within moments, Lily was escorted into a tall chair in front of wall-to-wall mirrors in a very modern-looking studio. A tornado of stylists started whirring around her in a cloud of dusting powder and setting spray. A tailor entered with a flouncy silver dress and asked Lily to try it on for size.

'I'll be back in a few minutes to make any necessary alterations. The Princess thought this would be nice on you,' he said.

Let's just say it was a transformation, but not the kind Lily had been hoping for. Lily looked at herself in a dress she had only ever seen in magazines, being fitted and adjusted by an expert team of tailors. At the same time a swarm of stylists hovered over her, finishing an over-the-top up-do. Someone had curled her lashes and added a pink glow to her cheeks. All topped off with a silver gown full of layers.

'Marvellous,' said the head stylist, walking in for one final inspection. He pirouetted before her, as if celebrating a job well done, and left. His team swarmed out after him in a cloud of spray and powder, the same way they had come in.

'I don't even know who I am,' Lily said out loud, looking at herself in the mirror.

And just when she didn't think it could possibly get any worse, Lily saw DJ, the Princess's cousin, walking past.

Lily wanted so badly not to be seen by anyone, let alone by a young royal with a snarky sense of humour. She would trade her ridiculous outfit and towering hairdo for the dorkiest hiking gear any day. 'What am I going to do?' she whispered to herself, hoping that the semi-frosted glass window would conceal her.

DJ walked past the room, but just when Lily thought she was in the clear, he did a double take.

'Looks like Pashmina's style team got to you,' he said, leaning against the door, hand in pocket. 'I'm DJ, Pashmina's cousin. I met you and your backpack earlier.'

As he continued to look at her dress, his cockiness seemed to fall away, to be replaced by a totally different expression. He looked sorry for her.

Lily did not know what was worse: that he should make fun of her or that he should feel sorry for her. But it was clear that he genuinely felt bad.

'Just want to say, I'm not bad with styling myself. I'm certainly better than Pash's gang, but don't tell her I said that,' he told her.

'I'm sure they meant well,' said Lily. 'I didn't want to interfere with what they were doing, but I didn't know that I'd end up looking, you know, so …'

'… like a wedding cake?' suggested DJ.

Lily burst out laughing despite herself. She really did look a bit like a wedding cake.

'I'd be happy to offer my services for free,' said DJ. The snark in his voice appeared to have gone. 'Truth be told, it really troubles me to see someone experience a fashion fiasco.'

'Oh, okay,' said Lily, not quite sure what to make of his comments. He certainly seemed much nicer than when they had first met.

'So, shall we try and fix this look?' said DJ.

'Yes, please,' said Lily.

Soon Lily's oversized curls and layered dress were given a modern twist. She now wore smart black pants with pockets and a formal white shirt that DJ picked out from the clothing rack.

'I've never worn anything like this, either, but I do feel more like myself,' said Lily, putting on a pair of boots.

'The only thanks I need is for you not to tell my mum, Lady Devi. She believes I should have more important things to do than save people from fashion disasters.'

'I promise I won't tell. I don't even know her,' said Lily.

'And just for that, I'll help you out with tomorrow's do as well.'

'Tomorrow? Another do?'

'Well, *duh*, this is Bagradoo,' said DJ, back in his usual element.

2

Too Much Gown

Status-hungry Lady Devi, DJ's mother, was all charm and charisma to the outside world. But behind closed doors she was carefully playing her cards to have her son DJ replace Princess Pashmina as the next-in-line to the Bagradoo throne. How DJ felt about this plan, Lady Devi hadn't asked, but she had on her side her most reliable and useful sidekick, the Island Minister Sir Vipin. Though as minister, he was the one with all the power, Sir Vipin somehow always turned into putty in her hands.

Lady Devi had a strong sixth sense and this kept everyone around her, even the Island Minister, perpetually on their toes.

That evening, Sir Vipin needed to give Lady Devi some information. It was not good news, and he planned to deliver it as casually as possible to get off lightly. Even with several rings on his fingers and a self-important air about him, Sir Vipin usually went from pompous to nervous the moment he was in Lady Devi's presence. It didn't help that he was hopelessly allergic to her perfume, causing him to sneeze in loud bouts, much to Lady Devi's irritation.

'Good afternoon, my lady. You look lovely,' said Sir Vipin with a little bow.

Then, in a single breath, he told her what he had come there to say: 'Just popped in to say hello. And oh, before I forget, I heard the strangest thing. You remember the half-moon pearl? Someone told me it was spotted at the bazaar this morning. Briefly, but then it disappeared again. The oddest thing! Anyway, are you looking forward to tonight?'

Lady Devi took a sip from her cup of tea, and slowly looked up. As usual, she was dressed in white, which she believed was her most flattering colour. Her lipstick was prominent, her nails were perfectly done and her hair was in its signature coif. All this served to make her look all the more intimidating.

'Did I hear you say that the half-moon pearl was seen today?'

'I know, would you believe it? Funny, right? Anyway …' Sir Vipin tried to move on as quickly as possible, but Lady Devi did not plan on letting him off the hook easily.

This was a big missed opportunity. The half-moon pearl was one of Bagradoo's royal boons—the first of twelve gifts of nature that protected life on the island kingdom. The half-moon pearl had the power to reveal all the remaining boons, but to do so it had to first be unlocked by someone in the palace. No one knew what the rest of the boons were, where they were or what mysterious properties they possessed. While the King of Bagradoo was known to have a scientific temperament and didn't really believe in lore and legend, it was an understanding by royal decree that if any of the island's boons were found, they were to be restored to the custody of the King, who would safeguard them for the protection and prosperity of the people of the land.

Legend had it that on this half-moon night of every year, the pearl would make a mysterious appearance on the island to make one single, heartfelt wish come true. When the time came, the pearl would glow, and whoever had it in their possession would have the opportunity to make their wish. As no one had seen the half-moon pearl in centuries, countless counterfeits had emerged in trinkets and charms every year, and the story had become the stuff of legend and celebration.

Lady Devi, however, was in on a secret. She had received a tip-off from an antique collector that the real half-moon pearl had been seen. If indeed the pearl made wishes come true, she would know what to wish for—the throne for her son. And she was willing to pay the antique collector a very big price for it.

Now, Lady Devi addressed Sir Vipin sternly. 'The half-moon pearl has been seen on this half-moon night and you are saying we don't have it? You are telling me someone else has it?'

'Ma'am, it was, in fact, to be a surprise for you,' said a crestfallen Sir Vipin. 'It is just that the person who was to give it to me told me there was an unexpected last-minute mistake.'

'Well done, very well done.'

Lady Devi's sarcasm made Sir Vipin stutter and grin in a comic-tragic sight. He proceeded to make frantic calls, juggling his three cell phones, sounding extra authoritative with whoever he spoke to. Soon, the antique store owner was presented before them.

'I don't have that pearl anymore, Ma'am. I had orders not to sell any half-moon pearls today but my nephew sold it to a tourist, although I told him not to.'

Lady Devi looked at Sir Vipin, her expression cold as ice.

'Finddd it. Tonighttt!' she thundered, exaggerating her consonants.

At dusk, Lily was in the balcony of her room, looking out at the dramatic scene before her. The sky went from blue to lavender and then pink, the clouds aglow from the setting sun. In an orchestra of chirping, birds returned to their trees in the lush garden below, where the fountain lights had just been turned on. The party music started to play, and a half-moon rose on the horizon.

Lily made her way downstairs to the ball and found herself in the middle of a dazzling party. With twinkling lights, music and tables of delicious bite-sized snacks piled delicately onto platters, the occasion was getting on to a royal start. Elegant guests streamed in, dressed in silver or white, the theme of the night. Princess Pashmina stood at a distance, surrounded by friends and fans waiting to meet her. Lily was awestruck by the spectacle, and grateful she was dressed appropriately for the glamorous night. However, she knew hardly anyone. To her relief, the Princess waved to her and walked over for a chat.

'Nice party,' said Lily.

'Everyone goes half mad on half-moon nights. It's mostly just an excuse to throw a party, so I can't complain. But the photo sessions can get a bit much; after a while, my cheeks start to hurt from all the smiling. So, I have to measure my smiles,' said Pashmina.

'You do have a lot of fans,' said Lily. 'Everyone seems so excited. Is there something special about tonight's half-moon?'

'There's an old tale that if you see this thing called a half-moon pearl on a half-moon night, there's half a chance that your wishes will come true.'

'Or half of them, at least?' joked Lily.

'You get the idea,' laughed Pashmina. 'I think I might start to half like hanging out with you!' she added, before wandering off to join her waiting fans.

Lily couldn't believe she had made a princess laugh. She didn't feel half as awkward anymore. It was time to eat some of that amazing food and shake a leg on the dance floor.

It was a long evening, and finally, Lily found herself back in her room, settling into her comfy pyjamas, typing notes from the day's incredible adventure into her diary. Moonlight filtered in through the window, and something on her bedside table started to glow. It was the pearl from the bazaar. The dusty little dented pearl shone bright, but Lily didn't notice it. She stretched, yawned and continued to write in her diary, trying to get cosy under the enormous silk and satin sheets.

Hi, friends of the Glog. It's been quite the first day at the palace. I can't say I made the best first impression. My backpack burst open in front of everyone at the palace and my roll of emergency toilet paper came streaming out. It was embarrassing. But then things got a bit better.

I saw this most amazing library of science books, and later, after a not-so-great fashion makeover, I started to mayyyybe make some friends.

The Princess's cousin turned out to be really helpful.

And the Princess too. Would you believe she even laughed at my joke at the half-moon ball?

Everything is lovely and out of this world, but does it make sense that I miss home a bit already? I mean, a lot. I can't believe I'm homesick. I miss my quilt ... Don't get me wrong, the silk pillows and covers are nice, but they're a bit too nice. I just wish I'd brought my favourite quilt.

Before she could finish her thought, Lily's quilt from her bedroom in Puddleton appeared before her eyes on her bed.

Lily froze in shock.

'Al? Al? Do you see this?'

'Hmmmm? Sorry, I have my eye mask on. Always do that right after flossing. Don't know about you but I've had quite enough of fireworks for one night.'

Lily peered at Al to see if he really had an eye mask on.

'Gotcha!' said Al. 'Sometimes the joke button just presses itself. Mrs Ray's instructions to keep you in good spirits when you get lonely.'

'Al please, I'm serious,' said Lily. 'It's just so weird how my quilt got here. I swear it wasn't here a moment ago. I didn't bring it. Or did I? Do you know? Maybe Mom packed it and then the room attendant unpacked it … though they didn't unpack my other stuff. It's just so odd …'

'Hmmmmmm,' said Al. 'I'm listening while not listening, you know, in the way that good roommates do. It's okay, you can keep talking. I might just dose off a bit, but you know I'll be there for you…'

And with that Al started to make gentle snoring sounds in the middle of which he muttered softly:

'They say that snoring, though traditionally considered to be annoying to others in the room, also induces a kind of calm and can have a soothing effect on them. The soothing power of a snore is sadly unacknowledged and underappreciated by human society …'

'Okay Al, switch off for the night, please. I think I'll just go to bed,' said Lily with a yawn. 'I'm just going to get under my quilt. I probably just forgot I packed it.' And with that she unfolded her quilt and snuggled into it. It smelled of home, and she immediately felt a soothing calm wash over her.

As Lily turned off her bedside lamp, the room went dark except for the moonlight, the palace lamp posts and the occasional fireworks still going off outside her window. But, unknown to her, something glowed, right beside her on the bedside table.

Lily gave another big yawn and pulled the quilt up to her chin. She was just about to fall asleep when she heard a tapping on the window. She peered at it in the semi-darkness. It sounded like a bird rapping its beak on her windowpane—almost knocking politely, as if to gently wake her. Lily turned on the bedside lamp and her heart stopped. This time, she could swear she saw the clear outline of someone's face. A face covered partially with a mask and a hat appeared outside her half-open window.

She opened her mouth to scream the loudest of screams, but before the first sound escaped her, the figure said, 'Shhhhhhh! Shhh shhhhhh, best not to scream, Miss. You'll wake everyone. Could you just hand it over.'

The strange person appeared to be suspended from a zipline. Lily thought quickly. As long as he stayed outside, she would feel okay. She did not want him coming in. So, she decided to talk.

'You can have it. My aunt sewed it for me, and I've had it all my life, but sure, you can have it. Why not,' she said, gathering up her quilt into a ball so she could throw it to the window and get this whole thing over with as quickly as possible. That scream was bubbling up inside her and was going to burst out any second.

'I will scream if you so much as *try* to come in. And I promise I will scream the moment you leave. I am just going to throw the quilt to the window, and you can catch it and take it away. Okay?'

'Not the quilt, Miss, that,' said the figure, sounding awfully polite for a thief as he pointed to the half-moon pearl on the bedside table.

'This?' said Lily. 'Oh, sure. I got it at the bazaar today. I don't even want it, so it's all yours. No need to pay me either, it only cost me a few dollars,' said Lily as she threw the pearl with surprising precision at the open window for the thief to catch.

'The half-moon pearl, Miss, is priceless. And tonight, it makes wishes come true. So, be careful what else you wish for. Actually, don't bother. It's mine now,' he added with a cheeky grin. 'Thanks! Great meeting you and I'm much obliged. I'm Strike, by the way. If you need something just call my crow, Kaw.'

Before disappearing into the half-moon night bright with distant fireworks, the thief turned around.

'Welcome to Bagradoo!'

He tipped his hat and, in a flash, was gone. A crow flew after him.

Lily was stunned into silence for a split second and then, in a delayed reaction, proceeded to scream. 'Thieffffffffff!'

Lily's scream brought the palace guards, maids and even Princess Pashmina and King Khair thundering into her room.

The King was dressed in a flowing velvet dressing gown. Even in the middle of the night, his beard did not look remotely tousled.

'Lily, are you alright?'

'A thief. That p-p-pearl.'

Lily pointed to the window, where a crow feather lay on the sill.

'If it is a crow feather, then it must have been Strike who visited you. Darned nuisance, that incorrigible thief. But really, he has never harmed anyone. Everyone has a Strike story, but he should have known better than to trouble a visitor. Robbing our guests of their baubles! He must certainly have given you a fright. Guards—catch him for once, will you! Darned nuisance. Good night, Lily—worry not, you are perfectly safe as our guest in Bagradoo.'

'You can stay in my room tonight if you like,' said Princess Pashmina, yawning a little.

'Are you sure? Maybe just for tonight …' said Lily.

A few minutes later, as Lily tried to fall asleep on the Princess's own double bed, thinking of what had just happened, she replayed in her mind what Strike had said as he left.

'Be careful what else you wish for.'

'You can say that again,' whispered Lily, wondering if she was right to have wished for the adventure of a lifetime.

3

Palace Pooch

The next day, in a decadent parlour in the palace, Lady Devi's face was covered in a smooth green paste spread perfectly over her cheeks, neck and forehead. Her hair was coiled up in rollers. She leaned back in her chair just enough to keep the cucumber slices on her eyes from slipping off, all the while sipping a green juice through a loopy straw. Trinket, her beloved terrier, sat at her feet, tracking Lady Devi's manicured fingers as she waved treats vaguely in his direction. No one dared disturb Lady Devi at this hour.

Except, that day, someone seemed to have mustered up the courage. Sir Vipin stood at the door with a large box in his hands, bursting with excitement and pride. He straightened his collar, examined his reflection in the glass door and knocked, unusually confident.

Lady Devi turned her head towards the door in disbelief. Who dared disturb her hour of calm? Everyone in the palace knew better. Even Trinket looked surprised at the audacity.

'What?' barked Lady Devi.

The shorter her sentences, the more threatening they sounded.

'Don't move an inch, Ma'am,' said Sir Vipin, as smoothly as possible. He sauntered over to the stool at her feet, kneeled and said, 'May I please' as he removed the fuzzy slipper from her manicured left foot. Lady Devi gave a nod, without disturbing the cucumbers on her eyes.

Sir Vipin then opened the flap of the large glass box he had brought along and placed her foot inside it. Try as she might to appear unimpressed, Lady Devi soon started to giggle uncontrollably. Something was tickling her foot.

'What on earth are you doing?' Lady Devi said, in between hysterical laughter.

Sir Vipin counted to one minute on his wristwatch and, when the alarm beeped, he slowly slid her foot out of the box.

'You might want to open your eyes for this, my lady,' said Sir Vipin.

Lady Devi finally let the cucumbers drop and straightened up, her eyebrows arching in an expression that said—*this better be really impressive.*

Smooth as velvet and decades younger than the right foot, Lady Devi's left foot looked a breathtaking symbol of travel back in time.

'Oh, my sweet foot … this is how you used to look twenty years ago … when I was the belle of the ball in Paris, in six-inch Louboutins … the apple of everyone's eye …'

Sir Vipin, looking incredibly satisfied with himself, strummed slightly on the box and whisked away the cloth covering, like a magician.

Inside was the strangest sight. Sloshing around in a few inches of water was a curious-looking creature, with the face of a baby terrier and the body of a sea horse. It was an adorable little animal, no bigger than the palm of a hand.

'Sea Ponypups, Madam, are found only in the forbidden cliffs of Bagradoo. They are so good at camouflage that they are only very rarely seen. Not this one though; a little too curious for his good. Ha ha ha! And here's the thing, Madam: there's much more to them then their cute blinking eyes,' Sir Vipin said conspiratorially.

'All you need for your skin to look younger for it to breathe misty puffs of its baby breath on you for one minute,' he further explained.

Lady Devi stood still, blinking. Her mind whirred.

'So, what do you think of your new pet? They are only good when little … any older than three months and they might just bite your toes off. Best to keep it as a pet for a few weeks and then get rid of it.'

Lady Devi looked up, eyes gleaming. 'Why would I want just one as a pet? I want a whole zoo. A breeding zoo. This is going to mean big business, fool. And oh, by the way, I need him right now to do my other foot. That way, I can wear my strappy heels for the party tonight,' she said, cooing to Trinket in a special voice she reserved just for him.

'Oh yes, certainly, Lady Devi,' said Sir Vipin, looking very pleased to have made himself useful to the intimidating woman. He, as the Island Minister, did everything in his power to please her, all in the hope that one day, he could rule the kingdom with her.

With her mint-new feet, Lady Devi headed to her shoe closet and brought down a pair of shiny kitten heels. 'What do you think of these?' she asked Sir Vipin as she squeezed into her old shoes, preening into the full-length mirror.

'Beautiful, just beautiful,' he praised as he took photos of her, though she looked quite comical with her hair in rollers, striking poses in shiny purple shoes.

Meanwhile, unnoticed by Lady Devi and Sir Vipin, Trinket and the Ponypup had struck a little friendship through the glass box. Both were curious and playful, and saw something familiar yet strange in each other's terrier-ness. Trinket was quite besotted by his new lookalike. Their eyes had met through the glass cage while Lady Devi and Sir Vipin were busy talking. Taking turns to frost the glass pane with their breath and playing pretend hide-and-seek, Trinket the terrier and the Ponypup soon became furry besties.

'What's the biz plan, the beeeeskneeeees plan—let's talk business!' sang Lady Devi, becoming excited, impatient and dizzy with the prospect of the fortunes to be made by selling the elixir of youth, one misty puff at a time. She would bottle

up the breath, like a miracle perfume, and sell it to thousands over the world like her who yearned to look younger and would pay anything for it. Of course, no one would need to know that it involved holding captive, in fine nets, a breeding zoo of tiny endangered baby Sea Ponypups.

'How do we get more of these? How?' demanded Lady Devi.

'It's quite simple, dear lady,' said Sir Vipin, basking in being the deliverer of good news, Lady Devi's favourite thing after macaroons and siestas. And money, of course. 'All I need to do is get the little critter back to the tidal pools on the forbidden cliffs. It is hatching season and as soon as I let him out of his box he is bound to lead me to the rest of his brood. In no time, we will have the nets ready and waiting for them—your on-site breeding zoo. The animals will remain where they are because they can only survive in natural tidal pools. I am told they won't be able to go anywhere either because of the fine nets that their entire nesting colony will be trapped in.'

'Get on with it then! What are you waiting for?' said Lady Devi, twirling in delight. 'They will survive just fine in cages. Net them, catch them and cage them, I say—this is big business.'

'As you say, Ma'am,' said Sir Vipin. 'I'll be on my way before the sun sets.'

Hot on the heels of his new best friend, Trinket, unnoticed by anyone, followed the Ponypup in Sir Vipin's box as he and his men made their way to the forbidden cliffs in search of more nesting colonies. The forbidden cliffs had got their name for a reason. They were steep, craggy, dramatic and windy, and the waters at the bottom were home to Sea Ponypups that lived in cold, dark, mysterious tide pools that few could reach.

Sir Vipin reached the top of the cliff and opened the box. Once of his men snapped an electronic tag around the little creature's neck and Sir Vipin went on to pour out the wet contents of the box, Sea Ponypup and all, over the edge of the cliff.

He sat back and watched a tracking device on his hand, following the little blue dot on the map as it zig-zagged its way down the cliff and stopped.

'That would be the spot, Sir. These little ones can never be alone; they always find their way home …'

Sir Vipin laughed wickedly, and proceeded to instruct his men to cover the nests in fine gauze.

Meanwhile at the edge of the cliff, unseen by anyone, poor Trinket, who had been following his friend all along, lost his balance and tumbled right down the craggy cliffs and splashed, unheard, into the waters below.

4

Royal Rescue

Hi, Gloggers!

Guess where I am this morning …

You got it. Bagradoo Palace!

Let's just say I had an eventful night … I can't go into the details, palace protocol and all.

But this morning, I made sure to take my gear with me as I went for a wander around the palace grounds.

The mornings here are magical … rays of sunshine … misty and warm air … peacocks roaming the grounds … and then there are the palace pondsssssssss! They are basically miniature habitats of what is out there on the island.

Also, look who I just met … An underwater creature, tinier than the tip of my finger. Meet Sea Bunny, everyone.

Have you ever heard of them? Their little sensors look like rabbit ears, and this tuft at the back looks like a fluffy tail–hence the name. Surprisingly, they are not in any way related to land bunnies, even though they too have fur of different colours. They only survive in these salty, shallow tropical waters, and the algae they eat have medicinal value. I learned all of this from Prof. Quill, the resident scientist who has been studying the rare species in Bagradoo and was kind enough to show me. He said I could share it on the Glog. I didn't tell him the Shlog also listens in, but he won't mind, I don't think. It's been a fascinating morning, and I haven't even had a chance to put my gumboots on!

'Paging Miss Lily for a makeover, paging Miss Lily,' an overhead voice on the palace intercom interrupted Lily.

Again? Oh yes, I've got to go and get myself party ready for another do in Bagradoo this evening. I'll be off, everyone!

A few hours later, at the makeup studio, Lily was faced with another fashion situation. Pashmina's team had her neck-deep in over-the-top high fashion. This time, the dress was pink with shoulder pads and matching pink boots. The makeup crew were busy adding layers of eye shadow, and her hair was piled up into what felt like an inverted ice cream cone. Once done, the crew swarmed out as fast as they had come in.

'Maybe I just won't look at myself in the mirror?' Lily grimaced, dreading what she might see.

Just then, there was a rap on the door.

'Hello, I thought I'd find you here,' said DJ.

'Hi DJ,' said Lily wryly.

'Woah,' said DJ. Lily expected him to laugh, but he didn't. Instead, he gave a brisk nod.

'Is it really that bad?' asked Lily.

'Well, let me just say if it was wedding cake last time, it's candy floss this time.'

Lily's face fell.

'Worry not—I don't have my online style degree for nothing. We'll tone it down while updating it at the same time.'

In ten minutes flat, Lily was already feeling like herself again. The candy floss pink dress top was now paired with blue jeans, sneakers and a fun sling bag.

'Thank you, DJ,' said Lily, ready to give him a big hug. He let her hug him only briefly before saying, 'Like I said, the only thanks I need is for you to tell no one. The best publicity for me is no publicity.'

A buzz of activity interrupted them as Princess Pashmina entered with her own style entourage.

'That's quite chic,' said Pashmina, giving Lily a once-over. 'It's not exactly per the brief I sent for you, but I like it. Don't tell me you brought that in your backpack!' she added cheekily. 'Hey team, check out Lily's look. Can you do something like this for me maybe next time? In fact, I've been hoping to change things up a bit. Actually, Lily, since you've nailed a great look again, let's make a splash together. Come on, help style me today … I had no idea you had this secret talent.'

Lily gulped and glanced sideways at DJ, who was stifling the biggest guffaw at the very big soup she seemed to find herself in. She had no clue about fashion and desperately wanted to tell Pashmina it was DJ who had helped style her. She looked at DJ again, and he gave the briefest of headshakes as if to say, 'Don't tell her it was me.' She knew she was sworn to secrecy.

'You look great … you don't need me! You've got experts so you're in good hands,' said Lily, trying her best to get out of the situation.

'Did you put together the look from a magazine?' asked Pashmina, getting straight to the point and refusing to be deterred.

'You know, I just looked up a blog here, a tutorial there … and put something together.'

'Ah, okay. Hey team, why don't we have Lily work on my look for tonight?' said Pashmina. This time, it sounded like an order.

Clearly, there was no going back. Lily had to style Pashmina!

DJ gave Lily a funny look as if he was buying front-row seats to watch the spectacle. To her relief, he then signalled as if to say, 'Don't worry, I'll help you out.' Was he going to use hand gestures like a secret game of charades? Lily was not sure how this was going to work but she had no better plans.

Pashmina's team rolled in a long clothing rack crammed with a crazy variety of clothes, in every possible fabric. Clothes made of velvet, suede, satin, organza, lace, etc., were available in all colours—green, neon, purple, turquoise, hot pink—and more patterns than she had ever seen.

Lily's head started to swim, and she looked through the clothes, trying to appear as confident as possible while trembling inside. She glanced at DJ, who seemed to be pointing with his eyes to something in the middle of the rack.

'Hmmmmm.' Lily pretended to do some serious fashion contemplation as she tried to find the exact piece that DJ was signalling towards. She placed a hand on a garment in the middle of the rack and looked up to see him nod. She pulled out a long, flared, bright orange pair of pants, quite like the colour of her life jacket when she went swimming.

The room fell silent. Lily looked up at DJ. He was desperately—with his eyes and chin—trying to tell her it was not the orange pants but the black ones. She finally understood and thought she'd casually replace the orange pants, as if she'd had a change of mind, but it was too late.

'Hmmmm, I think I know where she's going with orange,' said one of the stylists.

'Interesting …' said another.

Lily looked up at DJ again. He had to work with orange now, there was no going back. Pretending to scratch his ear, DJ signalled to a top. Lily touched it and looked at him again. He nodded. Tugging at the sleeve, she pulled out a hoodie with a giant bowl of pasta on it. The team stopped muttering and fell into a deafening silence.

'Just the fun, quirky touch she was looking for,' remarked someone.

'What about shoes?'

Lily looked at DJ, but he had given up trying to help and was just laughing silently, tears rolling down his cheeks. She went to the shoe rack and instinctively picked up the only pair that caught her eye—a pair of green gumboots with pretend laces painted on them.

Sometime later, there was Pashmina, the Princess of Bagradoo, wearing the most absurd outfit anyone had seen her in. It was most certainly a case of the princess's new clothes … with her entourage oohing and aahing for no reason.

'I read that the next season's trend is "wet weekend chic" and this look has that written all over it!' one of them said.

'Are you guys sure …' Pashmina trailed off. 'You're the experts, I guess.' She posed for a selfie and started typing in her hashtags.

Lily watched, eyes wide. This would be a PR nightmare if her look got out. Lily knew this was going to be the last time she would style Pashmina.

Suddenly, a chandelier-shaking scream pierced through the palace.

'TRINKEEEEET! WHERE ARE YOUUUUUU TRINNNNN TRINNNNNNN TRINKKIE PIE TRINKETTTTTT!!!'

'That sounds like my mum,' said DJ. 'Let me see what's going on.' He left the room and came back a few minutes later.

'Trinket has gone missing. Let's just say, Mum is hysterical.'

'Has he been gone long?' asked Pashmina.

'She's been looking for him for hours. She cooed high and low, and when he didn't show up for his favourite meal, she knew he was gone.'

Pashmina and Lily followed DJ into his mother's room.

Lady Devi was a bundle of nerves. Her cheeks were streaked with mascara and she was still in her dressing gown. If she wasn't quite so frightening in her panic, one would almost feel sorry for her.

'Send out a search party!' she bellowed into the phone to Sir Vipin.

'Right away, Ma'am,' came Sir Vipin's voice at the other end.

The palace security was summoned. The island was divided into a grid and the royal guards created a search map where everyone was allotted a square. The evening party had turned into a search party.

It was such an unusual site. Members of royalty were stomping around the palace grounds in their finery, looking for a missing pup. Echoes of 'Trinket Trinky … here here here' filled the air.

Lily combed every corner of her assigned grid, trying to find something. The stone, gravel and grassy areas showed no trace of the dog. Paw prints would be a great place to start, but the pebbled paths all around would not reveal any clues. Even if Trinket had been here, there would be no sign of her.

Lily decided to go further to see if he had left the palace grounds. Any real chance of finding Trinket would be before sunset, so there wasn't much time left. Lily came to the end of the tiered garden and finally saw a gravel path, crisscrossed by shoe prints and tyre tracks. She examined it closely on her hands and knees. Despite the path being freshly swept each day, she saw teeny tiny paw marks next to a set of shoe prints.

'I think I have found something!' she shouted, running back to Pashmina and DJ. 'I've found something.'

'I'll come with you,' said Pashmina, and DJ joined in too.

'I think the terrier was walking with someone.'

'I wonder who it was,' said DJ.

'I wonder where this path leads,' said Lily.

'This path leads to one place only, and that, according to this map, is precisely nowhere,' said Al the Pal from Lily's pocket.

'My thoughts exactly, but who just spoke?' asked DJ.

'Umm … it's my digital diary,' explained Lily, wondering how to make the robot in her bag seem more acceptable.

'Your own personal diary that talks? Like a pretend butler?' said DJ.

'More like a planner … with some extra features …'

'Okay then, whatever non-royals need, I suppose,' said DJ.

'Well, the path does lead nowhere, but that nowhere is also the forbidden cliffs,' said Pashmina.

'Who on earth would want to go there? There's nothing but rocks and cliffs and sludge,' said DJ, looking down at his once shiny shoes now covered in mud.

'Don't you wish you were in gumboots like me?' joked Pashmina.

'Well, I think we should follow the path,' said Lily.

'Are you serious?' said DJ. 'Do you really think Trinket would wander this far from her treats and favourite spot on the couch?'

'We've come all this way, we may as well look,' reasoned Lily.

'Heading southwest on an unmarked path towards an unnamed lane leading to what has consistently been called the middle of nowhere,' announced Al the Pal.

DJ looked amused. 'Well, if it's a pretend butler at least it has a sense of humour.'

The trio walked on for what felt like miles as the sun went down and most of what they could see was set in silhouettes. At times the path was slippery, at others rough and rocky. They saw some marine birds swoop low on the cliffs, but otherwise everything was silent. Hot springs popped up on either side at intervals, and wildflowers with sweet fragrances lined the path.

They walked on and on in silence until they reached the cliff's edge, with a dramatic drop below them. The choppy sea stretched out endlessly beneath.

'Well, this is a dead end,' said DJ. 'I certainly hope he didn't come here because there's no way we'll find him. He'll be gone for good if he's fallen in.'

'There's a reason these are called the forbidden cliffs. It's not forbidden by law to come here; it's just that common sense would forbid it,' said Pashmina.

They stood in silence, wondering if they had made a mistake coming out this far in the dark. And it looked like any minute now it was about to rain.

Lily was tired.

DJ was cranky.

Pashmina was pensive.

Just then, Lily saw a flash of light from a distant lighthouse. She followed it with her eyes.

'Yes, not a place one would want to fall into. But I still don't get why Trinket, who I'm sure loves his creature comforts, would want to come here?' DJ said.

'Hang on a minute,' said Lily, bringing out her binoculars and peering through them in the twilight.

In the distance, by the glow of the lighthouse, she spotted a movement in the water.

'Oh my god, there he is!'

A little white dog was paddling desperately on a piece of Styrofoam, struggling in the choppy waters to make his way to the shore.

'Trinket, Trinket—over here boy!' called DJ.

Trinket spotted them, and if puppies could smile, he certainly did. But try as he might to get closer to the shore, paddling furiously, he was getting nowhere. The currents were only getting stronger. Lily, Pashmina and DJ tried to clamber down the slope to get to him, but the cliff was too steep.

Just then, a loud cawing made everyone look up. Against the golden orange sky, a crow swept towards Trinket, picked up a long rope of kelp and brought it to the dog. Lily peered through her binoculars. 'Look, that crow! It is bringing a rope of kelp to Trinket. It is trying to tow Trinket to the shore! That's adorable. But oh no, the current's too strong.'

Pashmina, Lily and DJ were helpless.

Then Lily said, 'That crow, I've seen it before. It came to my window. I mean, it could have been any other crow, but it kind of behaved like a pet, like this one.'

A whistle sounded in the air, cutting through the noise of the crashing waves. There was a lone figure standing at a distance.

'Hey, who is that?' asked DJ. 'Look, the crow is bringing the kelp to him … and he's helping tow Trinket back.'

Trinket finally clambered out of the water, looking like a very wet pooch, shaking the sea water off his no longer immaculate fur.

The person who saved Trinket waved and walked over.

Lily froze. 'Pashmina,' she said, squeezing the Princess's hand, 'this is the person who stole my pearl, the thief who came to my room.'

'Oh, it's Strike?' said Pashmina. 'Catch him!' she said to the guards with her. 'He's never hurt anyone and usually gives away what he takes, but Dad wants him caught after he scared you,' she told Lily.

Strike saw the guards approaching.

'You might want to know that there's something fishy at the bottom of the forbidden cliffs. And it's not fish. Traps for sea creatures, I think, but I better be off. Au revoir,' he said with an exaggerated, comical bow. Before the huffing and puffing guards could catch up to him, the nimble Strike vanished into the dusk.

Trinket bounded to DJ and Pashmina, wet and cold. After shaking off the salt water, he started barking and walking away, as if he wanted them to follow him. He led them to the tide pool. There, peering up at them, were the little brown eyes of Sea Ponypups, trapped in a fine web of nets barely visible in the torchlight.

'What's going on here?' exclaimed Pashmina.

'What are these creatures? I've never seen anything like them!' said Lily, bringing out her camera to take a few pictures without scaring the strangely adorable creatures. 'They are the sweetest things I have ever seen. How could anyone want to trap them like this?'

'I'm not much of an animal person, but I have to admit those eyes are irresistible,' said Pashmina.

'After scanning their features, I can say quite conclusively that they are neither mammals nor amphibians, not fully furry nor scaly. So, in summary, I have no idea,' stated Al the Pal with an air of authority. And then he went on to say, 'It is a great feeling not to know, I might add. Less pressure than being an all-knowing non-being.'

'Uh okay, thanks Al,' said Lily as DJ and Pashmina cracked up.

'I think there is only one person here who will know what these are, and that's probably Professor Quill,' said Lily.

Later, back in the palace den, Quill looked closely at the photos Lily had taken of the tide pools and went rather quiet.

The King too was present; he, Pashmina, DJ and Lily all waited for Quill to shed some light on what the strange trapped creatures were.

Pashmina was getting impatient. She had a lot of other things to do besides waiting to identify a sea creature, even if it was rather adorable.

But Quill continued to say nothing. Instead, he slowly walked over to a part of the den partially hidden by a screen.

He emerged holding a large leather-bound book in his hands. The old and heavy book landed with a thud on his desk, sending up a plume of dust. Quill opened it slowly. He turned a few pages and ran his fingers over the finely calligraphed words before shutting it.

'Sea Ponypups from the forbidden cliffs, Your Majesty,' said Quill gravely. 'So well camouflaged are they that no one has seen them for decades. Their habitat itself is their protection. It is said their breath gives instant youth. I saw it before my eyes, years ago, when a fisherman caught one by mistake and brought it to me. Whoever has trapped them sees a huge commercial opportunity. What they don't understand is that no Ponypup will ever survive in captivity. Your Majesty, I think the Ponypups may be one of Bagradoo's mystic boons, a gift of nature.'

'A mystic boon? One of the supposed twelve?' said King Khair sceptically. 'I'm not sure I believe in the mystical boons, but these creatures look rare and in need of protection.'

'I agree with you there, Sir. Their youth-giving puffs of misty breath are certainly worth a lot to anyone who wants to trap them, but there is something I'm even more concerned about ...' said Quill. 'When a mystic boon is activated, it usually means the other boons will be too.' Quill's face looked grave. 'While I am happy that the mystic boons are alive and well, I am worried, Your Majesty. If they fall into the wrong hands, every one of these boons can be harnessed to terrible purposes.'

'I don't think there's any cause for worry, Quill. We will issue a warning that there will be no trapping of these creatures,' said the King. He sent for Sir Vipin.

Sir Vipin arrived with a self-important air. Yet, with the King, he was suitably deferential.

'Vipin, would you ensure that the forbidden cliffs are off limits. There are people trying to net the endangered creatures called Ponypups that live in the tide pools. No one must ever catch, rear or trap these incredible creatures. They are Bagradoo's natural treasure.'

'How strange, Sir, we will see to it that any such activity is stopped at once. The perpetrators will be found and punished to make it clear that anyone tinkering with life on the forbidden cliffs must be prepared to face the consequences.'

'Thank you, Vipin, I know we can trust you,' said the King. Sir Vipin exited the room with the air of somebody who felt he was the most important person on the island.

'So now, there is no reason to worry, Quill. We have it all under control with Vipin at the helm.'

'But Sir, what about the twisted force? Every mystic boon in the wrong, mischievous hand can be turned into a twisted force whose power we cannot control. Like the misty breath of the baby Sea Ponypup, while it gives you youth, it can be distilled into poisonous droplets with paralyzing effects.'

'I would draw the line at—what was that word—ah yes, the twisted something or the other.'

'Twisted force, Your Majesty,' said Quill, trying not to sound offended.

'Ah, yes. That's what I meant. No point in getting too carried away. But learn from Quill here, children,' said King Khair, turning to Pashmina, DJ and Lily. 'Learn from the older generation's work ethic, research, dedication and rigour. There are no shortcuts to diligence and hard work. He has spent years studying the natural life of our island. You should know this, Pashmina, because you too will rule the kingdom someday. When I am no longer here, you will be the Queen of your people and the island's treasures … they will be all yours to love, protect and cherish.'

'Yes, Dad, yes,' said Pashmina.

Lily couldn't tell if this was something Pashmina really wanted or not.

Dear Gloggers,

My day has been a dream.

A palace pooch went missing and a search party went out to look for him.

Imagine princes and princesses dressed for a ball, all stomping around among rocks and tide pools, looking for a missing pet.

I must say, it felt good to be part of something, and our good old swamp-combing technique from Puddleton helped me look for paw prints that lead the way.

The terrier, Trinket, is okay—a little cold and wet but so happy to be back home.

I better be off, I should be calling Mom.

Lily tried the "Mom" button on Al the Pal. It seemed a little too early in the morning for her to be up, so Lily left her a message.

'Hi Mom, I've had a really exciting day. We had an intruder in the palace. Apparently, he's known to not hurt anyone. He did steal something from my room though. Actually, he asked me to give it to him, and I did, but I'm fine. Don't freak out.'

The phone started to ring right away.

'Lily, I heard your message! Did you say you had an intruder? I think it's time you came home.'

'No, Mom, I'm safe. You can speak to the King's office tomorrow. I promise, I am so safe, I am sleeping in the Princess's bedroom! Please don't make me leave. I finally feel like I'm a part of things here at Bagradoo!'

5

Walkin' Wardrobe

'EEEEEEEEEEEEEEEEEEEEEEEEEEEEEEEEEEEK!!!'

The sound of Pashmina's scream awoke Lily from the best night's sleep she'd ever had. She was still sharing the Princess's ultra-luxurious bedroom.

'Pashmina, what happened?' a blurry-eyed Lily croaked as she peeked out from deep inside a plush duvet.

Pashmina was standing on top of the bed, pointing to her wardrobe. Everything was dark, except for two orange lights moving towards them.

'My wardrobe's walking!'

'Oh, so you guys call these wardrobe walk-ins, huh? Interesting. Back home we call them walk-in wardrobes.'

'What? What are you talking about? There. Is. Something. Walking. Out. Of. My. Wardrobe,' hissed Pashmina.

'Oh.'

It was true. A long gown from Pashmina's wardrobe appeared to be moving on its own, floating towards the bed.

'Let me get my torch,' said Lily.

'You actually have a torch?'

'Always sleep with it under my bed. An old camping habit, you know,' said Lily.

'Just as well,' said Pashmina.

Lily switched on her torch, and things started to become clearer. An enormous crocodile, wrapped in what looked like a very expensive green organza gown, was approaching them. Its eyes were orange.

'Did you see that?' whispered Pashmina to Lily.

'Aah, a crocodile wrapped in silk. Does that kind of thing happen all the time around here?'

'What? No, why would it?'

'You know, maybe because this is a tropical island palace and all.'

'The only tropical thing about my room is the custom wallpaper, Calm Palm.'

'I heard Queen Elizabeth had an intruder once, and apparently kept calm and carried on.'

'That's very helpful. Aren't you, like, an animal expert? Can you maybe do something?'

'Umm yeah, sure. I mean, in Puddleton we've studied dragonflies.'

Pashmina did not look impressed.

'And I did spot a near-extinct frog once. In fact, you might find it interesting. It's called the Blue Crowned frog. You know, crowned like royalty?'

'Riiiiighht,' said Pashmina, certainly not interested in any of Lily's nervous chatter.

Pashmina buzzed the bedside bell. A maid popped her head in, saw the crocodile's orange eyes, let out an even louder scream and then just slammed the door shut.

'Great. See, this kind of thing does NOT happen all the time in this palace bedroom, even if it is tropical. I'm calling Quill.'

Pashmina video-called him. 'Quill. There is a huge crocodile in my bedroom and I need it to leave right now!' she said into the phone.

'Ahh, I see, Princess,' said Quill. 'Now, until you learn the art of crocodile whispering or find someone who can persuade it to leave, please stay ten feet away, and don't make any sudden moves. And when you can, describe the creature to me in as much detail as possible.'

'It's huge, looks pretty nasty and is ruining my silks.'

'Right. And anything to help identify the species … subspecies, genus ideally.'

'Okay, here, see it for yourself.' Pashmina flipped her phone camera. 'I'd give you a closer view, but it does have about a hundred teeth.'

'No, no, please don't go any closer!' Quill shouted. 'I need you to identify it, safely.'

'Can I help?' said Lily. She studied the reptile's body and started to describe it in a slow, careful whisper. 'I see a lateral striation on its phalanx and a protruded anterior, low proboscis.'

'Ventricular movements … seems adaptable to a marshy habitat,' Al chimed in.

'Interesting,' said Quill's voice.

'Great, sounds like you all speak crocodile. Can you tell me what's going on?' said Pashmina.

They saw Quill move to sit down at his desk. A large book went *thud* on the table in front of him, and Lily and Pashmina heard him flip its pages. After a long silence, Quill looked up into the camera.

'It could be this rare amphibian with unnaturally bright eyes at night. They've only ever been seen at Adelen Lake. They never leave their environment, unless under distress. But now one of them is in your room. It must have come looking for somewhere cool and felt at home in your walk-in wardrobe.'

'Oh, it's feeling at home alright,' remarked Pashmina.

'I'll send the wildlife rescue team right away. Until then, stay on the bed and as still as possible. And the next time the croc snoozes, leave the room very quietly and shut the door. I, meanwhile, must go investigate Adelen Marsh to see why a monster croc would escape.'

'Ummmm, would it be okay if I came with you? In fact, I have this little gadget that tells me all I want to know about any species.'

'Okay, Lily, I hope you and your gadget can be ready to leave in ten minutes. Before the sun rises higher, we should be on our way.'

'Can't a robot get a little respect around here? I am not a little gadget, I am Al the Pal, the robotic diary + planner + scanner. I didn't think royals would struggle so much with my double-barrel name.'

'Sorry, Al, I know,' whispered Lily, and then wondered why she was apologizing to a robot.

6

Marsh Hellos

Lady Devi held an expensive gold teacup in her manicured hands, sipping her very early morning tea in bed. Her eye mask was pushed over her head, and her terrier slept next to her. She dialled a number on her phone and put it on speaker. The name on the phone said "V".

On the other end, a throat was cleared. 'Good morning, Lady Devi,' said a nervous voice, trying to sound casual.

'And …?' said Lady Devi, her voice so full of authority that anyone would feel weak in the knees if they heard it first thing in the morning. 'What's the status?'

'It's coming along well, Ma'am. It's almost drained. We should have the foundation ready in a few weeks and then the stores will see everyone filing into the world's most glamorous shopping destination—Devi Mall.'

'Aaaaah, I see you are a walking talking advertisement already,' said Lady Devi drily. 'Get on with it. And stick to the deadline. I am told the King is busy with an official tour. We want this done before he returns.'

'Yes Ma'am, certainly Ma'am,' said Sir Vipin.

Lady Devi could hear his toilet flush automatically. A mortified Sir Vipin tried to talk over it. 'Yes Ma'am, all in order.'

Lady Devi hung up the phone in mild disgust.

Lily and Quill left quite early. The sun had barely started rising as they got down from the jeep and walked towards the mouth of a river. A boatman was waiting for them.

'Lily, this is George.'

'Hello,' said George with a friendly wave.

'He is going to take us to Adelen Marsh. Very few people manage to find their way there. Even if they do, very few find their way back.'

'Oh really?' said Lily, her eyes wide. 'Why?'

'You'll soon see,' said Quill. 'But don't worry. With George, we're in good hands.'

Lowering their heads to avoid the thick branches of the trees at the riverside, Lily and Quill were helped into a boat by George, who wore rolled-up trousers, flip-flops and an old t-shirt. This massive adventure for Lily was just another day in George's life.

George had just started punting as Lily looked back to see the river mouth disappear, and thick foliage cocoon them. Soon, the hum of insects became so loud that it practically swallowed them up, growing louder as the boat made its way further down the water. To Lily, it sounded like they were surrounded by a swarm of dragonflies. But she couldn't see a single one.

She pulled out her sound recorder.

'This is loud,' said Lily, turning on the recorder. 'Friends, I am in a river in Bagradoo. Just hear this …' said Lily, speaking with her mouth really close to the mic.

'Pardon?' said Quill, and they both laughed.

Lily turned her mic outwards to capture the chorus of the insects. The humming was now so intense that it became the soundtrack to their meander deeper and deeper into the network of muddy river streams.

Finally, the sound faded, allowing them to speak.

'These channels of water are home to more mysteries than we will ever know. Life here is so protected by the mangroves that it remains an enigma to the outside world. People find the water channels impossible to navigate. A map drawn today will be of no use tomorrow, as the roots and branches of the trees can close in at any point,' Quill said knowledgeably.

'You can say that again. Maps don't help around here,' piped up Al.

'What was that?' asked Quill, a little perplexed by the strange voice.

'It's my talking planner,' said Lily. 'A digital diary that comes with maps and a voice.'

'I'm more than a diary, Lily,' said Al.

'Certainly sounds like it,' said Quill with a smile.

'Al has a background in science. My mom programmed him—she's a scientist.'

Lily brought out Al. 'Al does love plant and animal life. That's how he helped me tell you more about the crocodile.'

Al made a pleased buzzing sound. His mini scanner was now turning left and right, stopping at a low-hanging leaf and going in close.

'Heritierra fomes,' said Al. 'Wow!'

'Yes, that's right,' said Quill. 'That is one type of the many mangrove trees we have in Adelen. They are the lifeline of the island … their roots grow above the ground. They breathe in the air, and can even filter out salt. They literally hold the island together.'

'Hello, mudskipper,' said Al.

'Huh?' said Lily.

Al was now scanning a new visitor on the boat, a small frog-like mud-coloured fish.

As Lily reached out to put it back in the water, Quill said, 'No rush, these fish can breathe outside water. They walk on land. They even climb trees.'

'Woah,' said Lily. She could barely believe it and turned on her camera.

```
Gloggers, you have got to see this. Fish that breathe air. Fish that climb trees. I am not making this up. All thanks to this unique ecosystem that I am just learning about. And do you know there's more—
```

Quill interrupted. 'Lily, I must tell you, we need to be very responsible when we share our precious natural treasures with the world. I'm afraid as we get closer to Adelen Lake, I can't allow you to shoot more videos.'

Before Quill could say anything more, they heard a familiar sound. Though familiar, it felt strange, because the sound didn't belong here.

'What's that?' asked Lily.

'If it's grasshoppers then it's a new kind,' said George, trying to keep the mood light.

'I think that's the sound of people,' said Quill.

'Other people?' said Lily puzzled.

George punted forward slowly.

Between the hanging branches, a flash of bright yellow emerged, followed by the smell of diesel. Through the gaps in the leaves, peering through their binoculars, they could make out the painted yellow metal of machinery. Digger trucks, pipes, motors and men at work who had clearly been toiling in the cover of the night. There was only one thing they could possibly be doing.

'They are draining the marsh!' said George in alarm, letting out a low whistle. 'Sir, should I ask who they are?'

'No, George,' said Quill. 'These are not ordinary troublemakers. These people mean business and won't take well to being discovered. I need to find out who they are!'

Lily started to capture the scene on video. Meanwhile, George began turning around the boat, when the oar hit an exposed bark. *Thwack!*

One of the men looked up at the sound and signalled for the drilling to stop. As he squinted in their direction, Lily, Quill and George froze. Lily knew there was nothing concealing the boat but a low-hanging branch of mangroves. She wished she was back in the palace, better yet at home in Puddleton. Most of all, she wished that the man would not spot them, and that Al would know better than to make a joke out loud.

They were barely breathing when suddenly, there was another noise from the lake. A whole swarm of insects appeared like a green cloud. The machines had disturbed them, and they surrounded the men, who tried frantically to swat them away. If there was a time to leave, it was now. Without saying a word, George punted skilfully through the meandering muddy channels. It was the end of the longest thirty minutes of Lily's life.

'No humans following. Safe to speak,' said a robotic voice, making everyone jump.

'That's a helpful diary,' said Quill with a smile. 'I am relieved that we are out of danger, as you were here as my responsibility, Lily. But everything makes sense now. Adelen Marsh is being drained, which explains why the monster marsh croc made its way out of there. There will be reports all over the island of strange animals doing the same. We must stop the draining at once and restore the marsh to its natural state. Then, the crocodile in Pashmina's room can be captured and released.'

Back at the palace, an impatient Princess Pashmina waited outside her room.

'The animal rescue people have not yet managed to catch the crocodile. I need my room back!' she said crossly as Quill and Lily joined her.

'It's a monster marsh croc—very hard to catch, has never been done before,' Quill explained. 'But they are going to have to do it one way or another.'

'Yes, do something,' said Princess Pashmina. 'I have the entire team of *Isle Style* here and the fashion editor, Landon, is running out of patience. He's already been waiting three hours and has a flight for Paris tonight.'

Right behind her, a slender gentleman in a well-cut yellow suit and black-rimmed glasses was pacing in circles while talking to his assistants, who were pacing around the room with him.

'I see,' said Quill. 'But as your father is on tour, Princess Pashmina, I must tell you this urgent news. Somebody has made plans to drain Adelen Marsh.'

'I have some videos for you to see, if you'd like,' said Lily, bringing out her camera. Pashmina walked over and took a look, initially a little disinterested, but then more curious.

'We had to hide to record this because we didn't think they'd want us to see them,' explained Lily.

'But who are they?' asked Pashmina.

They examined the video closely: grainy, shaky images with men walking up and down, big bulky machines, earth movers and pumps at odds with the sounds of birds and insects. Then they spotted a clipboard with a diagram and some letters.

'There's something written there,' said Lily. 'Shall I try and zoom in?'

'Looks like a floor plan. Can you decipher the words?' asked Quill.

'... M ... A ... L ... L,' said Lily.

'Are they draining the marsh to construct a shopping mall in its place? I would be very surprised if the King granted permission for that,' remarked Quill.

'Oh, nice! So does that mean no more waiting for my online shipments to arrive by sea plane?' At Lily's confused look Pashmina clarified, 'It is such a chore to wait for online packages to arrive on the island, and they always get the sizes wrong. Then, I have to wait for the next plane to send the stuff back.'

'I'm afraid with the marsh drained, the only guaranteed parcels at your doorstep will be more marsh animals,' said Quill wryly. 'More monster crocs, and maybe the odd wild pig or flying cat.'

'And definitely mudskippers,' added Lily helpfully.

'You had me at crocs,' said Pashmina.

Lily felt a bit nervous. She didn't want the Princess annoyed with her, but it was true. She had witnessed the marsh's life and mystique firsthand.

'Pashmina,' said Lily. 'I'd love to show you some pictures I took. I know that to you, it's only your backyard, but for me and everyone else, the marsh is just magical.'

'If you say so,' said Pashmina, as she peered into Lily's camera.

The dense, dark forest, the hypnotic sound of crickets and the strange mudskippers appeared on the screen. Lily could have sworn that Pashmina was momentarily transfixed. But soon, the Princess regained her cool composure.

'So what am *I* supposed to do?' said Pashmina

'Princess Pashmina, you need to give orders in your father's absence that whatever is happening at the marsh be stopped at once,' said Quill.

'Okay,' Pashmina nodded. 'No mall, then. And I'd also like to return the croc in my bedroom.'

'Yes, that package came to the wrong address,' joked Lily.

Everyone chuckled.

'Nice one,' Al whispered to Lily.

'Thank you,' she replied, very pleased to have made the Princess laugh again.

It was time to check on that crocodile.

Having just woken up, it was now being lured with food by a team of experts from the zoo, who'd arrived to transport it back to the lake. They were trying to coax it to walk into an enormous wooden carrier by dangling wriggling fish on a fishing rod before it. But the crocodile, despite its size, was too quick for them, snapping up the treats in a jiffy.

'This has been going on for way too long. He becomes full after his snack and then falls asleep,' said Pashmina wearily. 'So not only is the photoshoot in my room hopelessly delayed, I've got Mr Teeth tangled up in one of my favourite dresses, and Landon has to leave for Paris tonight!'

'I have an idea,' said Lily.

All eyes turned to her, including Landon's, who'd joined their group and was now looking at Lily with an expression that said, 'A kid has no business having any say in this matter.' But now that Lily had started talking, she needed to pitch her idea.

'I think we can make the most of it,' Lily continued.

'Make the most of *this*?' said Landon, looking even more sceptical.

'I'm proposing a "Who Wore It Best" between the crocodile and the Princess.'

The room fell silent. Had she put her foot in it?

'That's the sound of crickets,' chimed in Al the Pal. 'Not the crickets at Adelen Marsh, but the sound of everyone not knowing what to say.'

'Thanks, Al,' said Lily, embarrassed. 'It was just an idea, since the crocodile is wrapped up in the dress anyway.'

'Sorry, can you repeat what you said, Miss?' All eyes turned to Landon. He was looking sharply at Lily over his glasses.

'You know … a "Who Wore it Best—the Princess or the Crocodile". Both of them are twinning in their green dresses,' she added softly.

Landon just stared at her in silence, and Lily wished she hadn't said anything at all. All eyes were on her. Then all eyes turned to Landon. Then all eyes swept to the crocodile. Then all eyes turned to the Princess. And then, they came back to Landon.

'I like it,' he said in a crisp French accent. 'A "Who Wore it Best". Let's do it. But we need a new dress for the Princess. A green dress, nothing else will do.'

'I think I know a designer who can help you,' said Lily.

'You know a designer?' asked Pashmina, clearly not believing it.

'Umm, yes, I do. In fact, he is in-house. Give me just one moment.'

Lily called DJ and asked if he would help. With the chance to style for *Isle Style*, DJ was all in. He knew his mother would be furious, but this was his big opportunity. DJ brought out all the dresses he had been making. As it turned out, there was more than one in green for the Princess and Landon to choose from.

The whole team jumped into action.

'May, I share a little sneak peek of the shoot on my nature vlog?' Lily asked Landon.

'*Oui*, I don't see why not,' he replied.

Lily pulled out her camera.

`My dear friends of the Glog, this is a slightly unusual Glog. Let's just say today has been an adventure …`

We returned safely from Adelen Marsh, only to come home to a monster croc that had accidentally wandered into the Princess's bedroom.

'Just to be clear, this kind of thing does not happen every day around here,' Pashmina added, appearing on camera.

Friends, I wish I could give you a closer look, but these giant reptiles are not meant to get close to humans. We need to get the message out that they are best where they belong … and that is in their lake. Otherwise, we might just have Monster Marsh Croc and his friends wandering into our wardrobes.

While we try to get the croc to leave, we thought we'd do a little contest to see who wore Princess Pashmina's dress better. We have before us the "behind-the-scenes" from the *Isle Style* fashion shoot … On one hand is the sleeping croc, wrapped in taffeta. On the other is the Princess in organza, styled by the in-house designer, Prince DJ.

So Gloggers, please vote and let us know who wore the green dress better!

The sleeping monster marsh crocodile looked majestic with layers of green taffeta draped over its scaly body. It was photographed in the backdrop of the Princess's walk-in wardrobe. Meanwhile, Princess Pashmina "twinned" with it in her own organza gown, accessorized with green boots and leaning against her tropical-themed wallpaper.

In no time, the behind-the-scenes pictures flooded social media with the hashtag #keepcalmandsavethecrocs. Online poll results started pouring in with votes and comments on who wore the green couture best. Lily's idea had been a huge success.

The whole island now knew that there was a rare crocodile in the Princess's bedroom because someone had disturbed the protected Adelen Marsh.

The men at work were soon tracked down, and it was revealed that Lady Devi was the one who had asked them to drain the swamp to make space for a mall.

That evening, Lady Devi came into Pashmina's room, gushing with exaggerated affection. 'Oh, darling Pashmina. I'm so sorry they let the cat out of the bag. I wanted to surprise you with a mall on your birthday.'

'Aunt Devi, I knew you had a generous side to you. Thank you, that was really sweet. But I'm afraid we just can't go ahead with it. What's the use of having gorgeous clothes if a croc outshines you,' she said, glancing at the poll results. 'The mall stands cancelled. But the great news for me is that I have my very own in-house designer in DJ! Just what I have been looking for. He has really kept his talent under wraps it seems, until today ...'

Just at that moment, the crocodile woke up, crawled out from under its cozy taffeta, took one lazy look at the writhing fish on the hook in the wooden box and calmly walked in, ready to be transported home.

'It's a wrap!' said Landon. 'Three cheers to you, Lily, for a great idea. Your name will appear in the photo credits.'

Lily was beaming with pride. It felt like she belonged, and that she had something to offer. 'Even if they sound zany, share your ideas,' her mother had always told her.

Back in a stuffy room in the palace, an elaborate old-fashioned phone rang. Sir Vipin's hand, bedecked in many gem-studded rings, answered the line. He'd been dreading this call.

'So that didn't go as planned, did it?' said Lady Devi's voice.

'No, my lady,' he said, clearing his throat nervously.

'To top it all, I had to behave all sweet and syrupy with that heir-head Pashmina. What humiliation! To have my son be her dressmaker ...'

'I do apologize, my lady. I had no idea that silly Quill and this most unexpected tourist would be travelling to the lake. It's all because of that vile beast which walked into the Princess's room.'

'Well, we haven't got all year,' said Lady Devi. 'Get cracking and do something, at once!' With that, she hung up, leaving the loudest ringing sound in Sir Vipin's ear.

7

Elephants Never Forget

King Khair, back from his tour, was huffing and puffing at the royal gymnasium. He had acquired the world's first VFX Rower, an outlandishly expensive piece of gym equipment that simulated a storm at sea. In a room dedicated to the King's new toy, a large sail flapped wildly as if caught in the roughest of storms. A projector in the background displayed a series of waves crashing while surround sound speakers blared the noise of winds and thunder. There were also mist fans spraying sea water. The King was perched inside a boat-shaped rowing machine that wobbled madly on a pedestal so he felt like he was being jostled around in choppy waters.

As the King heaved and grunted hard through the artificial storm, Pashmina and Lily popped their heads in. They had been asked to meet him at the gym and supposed, upon their arrival, that they had been invited to see this great new gadget.

'Sissies are they who exercise on stationary rowers,' the King declared. 'Anyone who has been at sea will know that the sea is never still. Anyone can row on a placid lake; the challenge is to take on choppy waters, I say.'

Pashmina and Lily couldn't quite suppress their laughter as they looked at each other.

'You're working hard, Dad,' said Pashmina.

'Got to lose a pound or two before the elephant parade,' said King Khair. 'Gaja just can't carry that one-ton Houda anymore.'

'Gaja?' Lily asked Pashmina, not sure who they were talking about.

'Gaja is Bagradoo's royal elephant. We love him. He has been with us for twenty-one years, carrying the Houda every year for the elephant parade.'

'The Houda?' asked Lily.

'It's a throne for the King, but one that can be mounted on an elephant. It's made of gold. It has all these carvings and cushions and looks pretty impressive,' said Pashmina.

Then, turning back to her father, she clarified, '*You* are losing weight since Gaja can't carry the Houda?'

Gaja, the King's favourite of the royal elephants, was now getting too old to carry the mounted throne, and a solution had to be found.

'Well, the Houda can't lose any,' laughed the King.

'PAAAAAAAARUMMMMMMMM.' An astonishingly loud trumpeting sound drowned out his last words.

'PARUMMMMMM,' the sound repeated, even cutting through the noise of the storm blaring out of the King's speakers.

'Goodness, what on earth is that?' asked Pashmina.

'Oh, here they are,' said the King jubilantly. 'I think you'll enjoy this. Meet my new elephant, Gaja the second.'

'Gaja … the second?' asked Pashmina.

'That's why I called you both in, my dears—to meet our new little Gaja. As you know, our Gaja the Great is getting a bit too old and will be retiring soon. This new jumbo will take his place—a new pet for you to pamper. I know you'll love him. He is from the same wild herd that Gaja came from. As you know, only one born in the wild can grow up to be strong enough to lift the Houda.'

Then, the King went on to sing his favourite childhood song:

'Only one born in the wild,
That drinks spring water as a child,
Dwells by the magic pond in spring,
Where wild lilies are blossoming . . .'

'And how do you get an elephant born in the wild to do the parade?' asked Lily.

'Worry not, my dear, our royal elephant trainers are adept at this. We get them young, treat them well and they become our pets. It is tradition,' reassured the King.

Lily was still taking it all in. A baby elephant brought in from the wild to the palace? She had so many questions. What about the elephant's mother? Did she come too? But how could one tame wild elephants? Surely, they must be better off in the wild?

But before she could say anything further, in came a trumpeting, hot-tempered baby elephant. Five men tried to control it, but the calf would have none of it and started lashing out, desperate to escape the ropes it was tangled in.

'I don't speak elephant, but I think it's saying it doesn't want to be here,' said Lily.

'Yeah, if I had to take a wild guess, that would probably be it too,' added Pashmina.

'Oh, sentimentality! Do you think I'm some sort of heartless old tyrant? We trapped him humanely and we will treat him grandly. He will have other elephants to play with and will hopefully befriend Gaja, who will teach him the ropes.'

'Ropes … yup, you can say that again,' said Lily.

'He will be treated to the tastiest meals—the freshest grains and jaggery hand-fed to him every morning. Mahouts will give him luxurious baths. He even gets to swim in the royal estate ponds and frolic on our grounds. All in exchange for carrying me and the Houda around town once a year, in the years to come—a fair deal I would say. Off you go, little champ, you'll feel at home in no time …' The King patted the elephant on his head.

At those orders, the stable hands of the mahout coaxed the elephant out of the room. His trumpets faded into the distance, but not his spirit. He was going to give his caretakers hell alright. Soon they heard the—not exactly unexpected—sound of something crashing. It sounded like a cabinet of china.

'I hope that wasn't my mother's beloved porcelain,' said the King worriedly.

'How did they bring him in from the wild?' asked Lily, truly astonished by what she saw.

'Oh, I think it's a big forest picnic party … yes, back in the day didn't they have those forest picnic parties?' Pashmina said.

'And the baby elephant became part of that … how?' Lily wanted to know.

King Khair chimed in. 'Tradition, custom, history … Pashmina, it's time you learned more about Bagradoo's traditions, my dear. Don't you want to be part of what makes our island great? The pomp and pageantry? One day, my dear, you will be the Queen, sitting on the mounted throne, carried by Gaja who leads the elephant parade.'

With that, he burst into another song:

'Gaja the great, descended
From a line of famous tusks,
For seven generations, carrying kings,
Without a huff or puff.
Ninety golden kilos is what
The royal Houda weighs,
And on festive days, it's always Gaja,
Who is the star of the parade.
But every twenty years or so,
Comes the fateful day,
When the King's great ride is deemed too old,
A younger one must be found and told,
Just how to be the new big thing,
To flaunt and flatter the Bagradoo King.
Since no haathi born in the palace stable,
Is ever strong enough to bear,
The kings' gold and purple Houda,
One that is passed from heir to heir.
Only a calf born in the wild,
That drinks spring water as a child,
And dwells by the magic pond in spring,
When white lilies are blossoming.'

'So they caught one from the wild?' asked Lily.

'Oh yes,' said the King. 'And this is how it went.' The King sang and showed them some pictures on a projector screen:

'Deep into the forest marched
Drummers, trumpeters and noisemaking men,

All set to make a noise so loud,
That bees would scatter, and deer would bound,
And crickets would sit without a sound.
Once the birds had fled with all their flock,
The wild elephant herd ran all amok.
Then tripped by a string of silken hair,
Invisible by the waiting lair,
Into a ditch of leaves and mud,
A young guest landed softly, thud!
The drop was steep, about eight feet, but wounded he was not,
I had given orders to make sure the trap was soft.'

'Here he is, Pashmina, Gaja the second, the seventy-fifth to succeed those from his herd. He has come to the palace fresh from the wild, ready to carry the golden throne. I am so glad you were here to witness this historic occasion.'

Lily stood there in confusion, not sure what to make of her feelings. She respected tradition, but she was not okay with this—not a baby elephant being separated from his mother! No, not under any circumstances. Lily looked at Pashmina as the two girls left the room. Surely she, like Lily, felt terrible for the poor baby elephant.

No longer able to keep it in, Lily said, 'Pashmina, I just can't get over that poor baby elephant. I mean, what if he has a mother who is missing him?'

'I know, poor chap,' said Pashmina. 'I felt really bad for him too. We've always had elephants, but this is the first time I've seen one brought in from the wild.'

'Do you think … maybe …' ventured Lily.

'Maybe what?' said Pashmina.

'Maybe we could find a way to …'

'To?'

'Maybe we could find a way to reunite him with his mom,' blurted out Lily.

'What! How?'

'I don't know, maybe we could take him back …'

'Take him back? They won't let us do that.'

'I know … but he can't be forced to stay here. He will be miserable for the rest of his life. I know you don't like it either, Pashmina, so let's just find a way to … take him back.'

'But he's here now, and no one will agree.'

'I know, but he is helpless, and no one will help him but us. So we'll just have to …'

'So, you mean like …'

'Yes.'

'Really?'

'Really.'

'We kidnap him,' they both said together.

'I thought you'd never say it …'

'We'll have to take matters into our own hands,' said Pashmina. 'It's either that or sit around doing nothing while Parumm is separated from his mother.'

'Parumm?'

'Yes, with all that trumpeting, I can't think of any other name for him.'

'Parumm it is,' said Lily with a smile.

Lily felt the anger and sadness that was welling up inside her slowly subside. She was so relieved that Pashmina felt the same way about the elephant.

'So, how are we going to do this?' said Lily.

'You mean, how do a teenage princess and a twelve-year-old blogger pull off an elephant heist?' said Pashmina, laughing.

'Yes,' chuckled Lily.

'We need to win Parumm over and let him know that we are his friends. But how? I bet he hates all human beings. How can he trust us after all that we have done to him?'

Lily agreed. 'We need someone he can trust. Someone *we* can trust. Someone who knows how elephants behave and who won't tell on us.'

'Moss,' said Pashmina.

'Who?' asked Lily, puzzled.

'Moss, the elephant keeper's son. He's just a kid but he has this deep bond with elephants. They call him the elephant whisperer. His father is Gaja's carer.'

'We need to meet him right away.'

'I have a headache, please clear my afternoon calendar,' ordered Pashmina into her phone. When she had hung up, she whispered to Lily, 'They won't believe that I'm off to the elephant stables. I haven't been there in years, not since I was six and, apparently, totally *obsessed* with elephants.'

Lily followed Pashmina outside the palace, where everything was moving at a glacial pace in the afternoon heat. The trees and topiaries cast long shadows in the overhead sun, and even the birds weren't chirping. People dozed or stared off into space, and the guards made idle chatter—it was too hot to be on any kind of alert.

Pashmina and Lily kept to the shade of the trees as much as possible. Lily was quite impressed with Pashmina's stamina; she herself was exhausted and sweaty from the afternoon heat. They finally arrived at the stables.

Inside, the air was heavy and still. In a shallow, cool pool, Moss, a young boy of seven, was relaxing on the back of an elephant having a long bath. Lying back with his eyes shut, Moss was clearly enjoying the occasional spray of water along with a gentle sway of cool air from her enormous flapping ears. All in all, this for him was a perfect summer afternoon.

'Good afternoon,' said Pashmina, marching into the elephant stable like she owned the place. Well, she kind of did, but still. Everyone stirred from their afternoon stupor.

'Good afternoon, Princess,' said Moss's father, the elephant keeper, who had expected to see anyone but Princess Pashmina. However, being a dignified member of the royal retinue, he knew better than to show his surprise. Members of the royal family were free to come and go anywhere at any time. 'How may I help you today, Your Highness?'

'I'd like to speak to Moss,' said Pashmina, looking up at the boy, who was now humming and chewing on a piece of straw while simultaneously encouraging the elephant to spray him with more water.

'Moss … Moss!' said his father. 'Can you please get down here?'

'Not for love or money,' said Moss.

'Moss … you need to come down here,' his father insisted, in as calm a voice as possible. Moss yawned. 'My executive assistant handles all changes to my schedule,' he replied cheekily.

'Moss, I think you should reconsider.'

At his father's serious tone, Moss opened one eye. When he saw the Princess, his eyes widened in surprise, and he almost fell off his perch. He would have dropped to the ground with a thud had it not been for the elephant, who gently stopped his fall with her trunk.

'Princess Pashmina … what are *you* doing here?' said Moss, expressing all the shock that his father had tried not to.

'We need your help, Moss. Now. And it's a top secret,' said Pashmina, with a cool air of authority. It looked like she knew exactly how to get Moss interested.

'I'm all in,' said Moss. It was not every day that a princess came to the stables, let alone ask for him specially!

Pashmina, Moss and Lily gathered for a little round-the-hay conference. It was clear that Moss's father was not invited to be in on the plan. Not yet, at least. A plot was hatched. Moss would befriend Parumm, like he did with all elephant calves born on the palace grounds. Only this time, it would be a challenge because Parumm was born in the wild and did not have his mother with him. This baby elephant was scared, angry and homesick.

Moss thought about it for a bit. The only way to win over the elephant was to play with him. 'The first game I'm going to play is shadow,' said Moss with clarity. Pashmina and Lily liked the sound of that. Moss would copy the body language of baby Parumm as if he were his shadow. There was no better way to win the little one's trust than to mirror his moves with playful games. Then Moss would try to switch roles and get Parumm to shadow *him* as part of the game.

'Oh, now I get it …' said Lily, 'you are going to do that to get Parumm out of the stables!' She was practically jumping in excitement.

'If I sneak out of the stables at night without making a sound, he might just do the same.'

Pashmina, Lily and Moss charted out the entire plan in detail.

Moss would walk into Parumm's stable and try to befriend him with a few treats, including every elephant's favourite—the berries of the Falsa tree that are only found in the deep forest in summer.

He would proceed by giving him little balls of molasses. If that put the baby elephant in a good mood, Moss would start the game of shadow. First, he would shadow Parumm. Then, if things went well, Parumm would shadow Moss. Moss would then creep out of the stables at night, with Parumm following him silently.

'I've got this,' said Moss. 'Your wish is my command, Princess Pashmina and Miss Lily.'

Once it was clear that Moss knew what he had to do, Lily and Pashmina left the stables.

'We now have something we must do,' said Pashmina. 'And I will need your help.'

'Whatever you say,' said Lily. 'Whatever it takes.'

And so the plan unfolded …

That night, when everyone was fast asleep, Moss untied Parumm. A few treats later, Parumm was in a better mood, and Moss started to shadow him. The baby elephant was delighted to have someone to play with and started swaying from side to side, enjoying the comic sight of a little human playing the shadow game with him.

Finally, by nightfall, after Parumm had his meal, and a little rest, Moss decided to turn the tables to see if Parumm would copy him. He started to tiptoe around, creeping slowly in circles and then towards the arched doorway. He wondered if Parumm would follow him and if the baby elephant could be as quiet as a mouse. One glance at Parumm and his worries vanished—the animal walked behind him just as soundlessly.

Moss hoped in his heart that no one would stop them as he passed the first stable guard, who was fast asleep. With

Parumm following him, Moss then walked past Gaja's own stable, where Gaja snored softly, his enormous body quivering. In a few moments, they were outside the stables and at the edge of the forest.

The forest was aglow in the moonlight, and the air was heavy with the scent of night jasmine. One could hear the hum of insects and the hooting of the occasional owl. The grass felt soft underneath Moss's feet. Between the branches of trees, the brightest of moons shone in a dark blue sky sprinkled with stars.

Meanwhile, back at the stables, Lily and Pashmina walked into Gaja's courtyard, a large and airy space which smelled of fresh hay.

'Are we really doing this?' said Lily.

'Yes,' Pashmina assured her. 'We have no choice. We can't leave Moss alone in the forest. What if something happens to him? We can't tell Moss's father; it would get him into too much trouble. The best thing for him is to not know; that way he won't be guilty of breaking the rules or betraying the King. It will be easier for them to forgive seven-year-old Moss and us!'

'Good thinking, Pashmina. Don't worry, I'll help you,' said Lily. 'You can do it.'

'But how do I get Gaja to listen to me?'

'Remember you said when you were six, you used to come to the stables all the time? What were some of the games you played with him?'

'Well, I would basically come here for my afternoon siesta and evening ride. We'd eat sugarcane together.'

'Great!' said Lily. 'Elephants have a great sense of smell and memory. I am sure Gaja will remember you by your scent, even if he can't see you in the darkness. Remember, an elephant never forgets.'

Pashmina walked carefully into Gaja's stable. The elephant was still fast asleep. As she walked closer, his snoring got softer and then slowly stopped. He seemed to stir as she approached.

Pashmina looked back at Lily. 'You can do it, Pashmina ... go closer,' whispered Lily, smiling. She tried to sound encouraging, though she was terrified herself—not just of breaking palace protocol but also being so close to an enormous elephant whose caretaker was fast asleep.

As Pashmina went closer, Gaja stirred some more. She gently touched his head. His eyes remained shut. Taking a leap of faith, she curled up next to him. As if by instinct, the elephant tucked her closer to him with his trunk. Then, Gaja opened his eyes—he recognized Pashmina. Lily's heart stopped for a moment. This was going just as she had hoped but it was terrifying all the same. What if Gaja was upset at not seeing her for all these years? What if it made him confused?

But Gaja wasn't confused or upset. He welcomed Pashmina like he had done when she was a child, by patting her head with his trunk. She smiled and gently tickled his ear, stroked his forehead and gave him a big stalk of sugarcane.

She then whispered in his ear. 'Wake up Gaja, please, I need your help. But please be quiet.' Lily's eyes widened. Pashmina could speak to elephants? She was not just a princess of organza dresses, fashion and fan-following?

Gaja did as Pashmina asked. He slowly sat up and then started to stand, a process that took a few minutes. He then swooped Pashmina onto his back. As they walked over to Lily, Pashmina whispered something to Gaja. Gaja scooped up Lily too and quietly padded out of the stable while his keeper continued to snore softly.

'You did it, Pashminaaa!' exclaimed Lily. 'You did it!'

Pashmina smiled. 'Thanks, Lily, I really didn't know whether I still had it in me, if I still had my bond with Gaja.'

Meanwhile, deeper in the forest, Moss kept on walking, knowing his way in the moonlight. Parumm followed him, copying Moss's dance steps. But Moss knew Parumm would stop the game the moment he smelled the scent of home.

Sure enough, as they reached the very spot where Parumm had been caught, the baby elephant stopped and started to—true to his name—trumpet. *Paarummmmmmm.*

Suddenly a bigger, louder trumpet shook the air—it was Parumm's mother and the rest of the herd. The trumpeting got louder, and an angry elephant came charging towards Moss.

'Run, Moss, run!' shouted Lily. They had reached just in time. Moss ran as fast as he could to Gaja, who swept him up with his trunk and placed him on his back with Pashmina and Lily.

On seeing Gaja the Great, estranged yet one of their own, the rest of the elephant herd stopped. They looked at him and trumpeted in unison, a sound that meant both hello and goodbye. They respected him and would not charge one of their own, even if he was no longer with them. With Parumm safely at the centre, the group started to walk away. The baby elephant looked back just once, to see Moss, his friend, for the very last time, before his mother placed her trunk over his head. The gesture revealed her single, short, sharp tusk, glinting bright in the white moonlight. She had her baby with her and would not allow anyone to ever come close to him again.

8

Flying Throne

That night Lily journaled.

Pashmina and I broke the palace rules, but for a good reason. Although I do have a feeling we are going to get into trouble. Do you know that wild elephant herds have family bonds for life, and they recognize their family even if they have not met in years? And that a mother elephant will do all she can to protect her baby.

Lily could barely sleep all night knowing that Parumm's absence would be noticed first thing in the morning, causing chaos in the palace. In the early hours before dawn, just when her exhausted mind and body had fallen asleep, she was woken by loud voices outside the room. Pashmina and Lily went to check what was up.

Quill had come thundering into the palace apartment in a panic, something quite unlike him. Pashmina did not look pleased that she had, once again, been awoken before time. King Khair had joined their company in his velvet robe, his perfect white beard still intact.

Quill started muttering to himself. 'I am sorry to disturb you like this, Your Highness, but … but … in the fifty years that I have been here in the palace, not a day has passed when I have not seen the Ledger on my desk when I walked into my den. I thought that no protection was the best protection, that no one would care if it was just there, unlike the royal jewels under lock and key and maximum security …'

'Quill, calm down. What happened?' asked the King.

'The Ledger of Boons, Sir. It's missing!'

Lily let out a gasp and looked around the room. No one else seemed horrified.

'The Ledger of Boons?' asked Pashmina. 'It's just a book, I'm sure you'll find it.'

'The book has been in the family for a few centuries, marked with the royal seal going back thirty generations,' said Quill.

Lily gasped again. She had never heard of anything going back more than two generations in her family. She had her grandma's recipe book and photo album, but beyond that, she had no idea who anybody was, let alone have a book with their names or seals in it.

'Sir,' Quill said, addressing the King with the air of someone about to give a very solemn speech. 'When I first arrived as a traveller to Bagradoo, you kindly offered me the chance to study the Ledger. You knew of my work with rare species and of my interest in old records and texts. You felt that I could be trusted to decode the Ledger's secret language and preserve it for future generations. You entrusted me with that job. I worked for long years to decipher the language and found that life on the island was, in fact, protected by rare species found nowhere on the planet but here. Species that can protect the people and the land. If this information reaches the wrong hands, Sir, there is no telling what can happen …'

With this speech, Quill lost his composure and started weeping.

'Let's put up a poster announcing a reward,' suggested Lily. She really found it hard not to offer help where she could.

Al jumped in too: 'It's outside my usual work hours, but I could draft one for you—I have the template of the missing puppy poster from Puddleton. How about we change the word puppy to Ledger?'

Quill said, 'The best preservation of the secret was that no one had the patience to learn the language and decode the mysterious web of life on the island. So, the Ledger was always safe here, safe because no one cared to delve into it. I'm afraid that announcing we have lost the Ledger would bring out all kinds of mischief-makers who will now want it.'

'Okay, so we include a warning,' said Al impatiently.

'Whoever stole the Ledger,
Be prepared to be cursed;
Unless you bring it to us,
And 'fess up to it first.'

'Good rhyming from your robot friend, Lily, but imagine what could possibly happen if the book falls in the wrong hands. While I'm sure the good people of the island would help us find it, we already know what's happened at the forbidden cliffs and Adelen Lake. There are people out there who do not understand how delicate the island is,' said Quill.

'Quill,' the King spoke at last, 'are you sure it hasn't just been misplaced? Where was it when you last saw it?'

'In my den, Sir, always in my den. It never leaves my den.'

'Let's have a look,' said the King, and together they all trooped downstairs to Quill's den.

The study was in chaos. Only one person could navigate the place, knowing exactly where everything was.

'I assure you, the mess is not the problem,' said Quill to King Khair, who was surveying the clutter on Quill's table.

'I tell you, it is possible the mess *is* the problem,' the King retorted, and the two bickered like old friends.

'You just don't know where you put the Ledger, so it's more likely to be missing than stolen. Or someone is just playing a joke on you.'

'Wishful thinking, Your Majesty … wishful thinking. If anyone got their hands on the Ledger and wanted to make mischief, they'd be able to do it alright. I dread to think of it. Our island, our future, our mystic boons, the gifts of nature—they would want to use those gifts for profit, or worse. What if they unlock the twisted force? I can't even fathom …' Quill started muttering to himself in a full-blown panic.

'But I thought you were the only person who could read the language, codes, diagrams and formulas,' said the King, trying to reassure him.

'I am, I was, or I thought I was, but how can we be sure, Your Majesty? Who knows? Someone somewhere can find some secret way to decode it all.' Quill started to look around his den and reshuffle things.

'Calm down, Quill,' said the King. 'Calm down. No one but you has glanced at the Ledger for years. Why would they want it now?'

'It is the year when, according to the Ledger's almanac, the half-moon pearl will appear on a half-moon night, unlocking nature's mystic boons. This means, Your Majesty, that it is possible for all the boons to come alive. Their force could make the island thrive or cause havoc if this energy is twisted.'

'Come, come now, let's not get ahead of ourselves. I have a parade to lead, one of my last parades with Gaja. Would you believe I've lost six pounds?' said King Khair, attempting to change the subject.

'Very good, Sir, very good,' replied Quill, trying his best to seem composed.

'It's time to prepare Gaja for the parade and to share with my people that there is going to be a new Gaja, Gaja the second,' continued the King.

'Ummm …' said Pashmina. 'About that …'

The King looked questioningly at her and Lily.

'We have something we need to share with you, Dad,' said Pashmina. Lily held her hand in support.

Together, they recounted the entire story to the King. They told him how they felt when they saw Gaja the second angry and scared. They told him what they planned to do, and how they got Moss to help. They told him how Moss's father had nothing to do with any of it. They also told him how happy the elephant's mother was when her calf came home. And they told him about the strange, awe-inspiring moment when the domesticated, royal Gaja met the rest of his wild herd.

The King just listened. At first, he said nothing, but then he laughed, clapped and patted Pashmina on the back. 'My dear child, you have proven that you have your own vision for the future of our kingdom.'

'What use is tradition if it isn't kind?' said Pashmina.

'True, my child, true, but who is going to carry the Houda now? The people will still want to see it, even if Gaja is not carrying it.'

'I have an idea,' said Lily.

It was the day of the annual elephant parade, and all of Bagradoo was excited. Little children, enjoying their day off from school, lined the streets, which were decked in colourful flags and streamers. The star attraction of the parade was always the smiling Gaja, great and large enough to carry the King seated on a one-ton throne. Everyone loved this majestic elephant—born in the wild, now the pride and joy of the people and the palace. Swaying from side to side, he did the rounds of the town with people showering flowers and confetti on him. This was an annual tradition and huge crowds had gathered to witness it, knowing that in a few years, Gaja would be replaced by another calf born in the wild.

Little did the crowd know that behind the scenes, something else had been brewing. Lily and Pashmina had hatched a plan and they were hoping to be able to pull it off.

The opening band entered through the canopy-lined lane, greeted by rows of excited onlookers. The drummers were then followed by the King's finest horses. Vintage cars followed suit, and after the last car in the royal fleet was greeted by eager crowds, everyone waited with bated breath for the newest addition to his collection. This time, it was his boat—all ready for retirement, brought out on a wheeled float.

The excitement of the crowd gave way to hushed anticipation. Then, the pipes started with a familiar tune of "Here Comes the King's Elephant", Bagradoo's beloved island pageant song. The theme music had been played year after year when the King appeared on the Houda, swaying on the back of his biggest elephant. As the music grew louder, the crowds started chanting in a chorus, 'Gaja, Gaja, Gaja, Gaja'. The chants grew louder and louder, but there was no sign of Gaja. Kids in the crowd craned their necks, wondering why Gaja had not yet appeared. The chants started to get more and more restless, but still there was no sign of Gaja. Lily and Pashmina looked at each other, steadying their nerves. This was the moment; if they could get through it successfully, all would be well. Then, just as the music hit its peak, there was a shower of flower petals from above. Everybody looked at the sky.

An elephant-shaped hot air balloon was flying in the sky, carrying the Houda. King Khair sat on the throne, flying high up in the sky. The hot air balloon was decorated and painted to look exactly like Gaja. Pashmina and Lily wondered if the crowd would like it.

And then Gaja emerged before the crowd, free of tethers, just as himself, no heavy one-ton Houda on his back. He was decked in a soft piece of cloth and a garland of flowers, leading a parade as he had always done.

How would the crowd react? In the next three seconds, Lily and Pashmina got their answer.

Three, two, one … 'Hurrrrrrraaaahh!'

The crowds went wild. They waved to the drone cameras that captured their delighted faces, broadcasting them live on

two columns of TV monitors. The zeppelin descended, and the King dismounted. Gaja, tall and majestic, was there to greet him. The crowd gasped collectively at his swaying walk, exclaiming, 'Woahhhh!' The King met his beloved elephant and as he stroked him lovingly on his forehead, Gaja curled his trunk around him in an embrace, making the paparazzi snap away madly.

The live TV coverage discussed why the King had stopped the royal tradition of a mounted throne, effectively ending the custom of taming elephant calves born in the wild. On the screen, the anchor was heard announcing, 'And to quote the King, "What use is tradition if it is not kind?"'

Pashmina beamed. *That was my line, Dad, but that's alright—you can use it.* She and Lily couldn't believe their plan had gone this well.

The cameras panned to the hovering zeppelin that represented everything new about Bagradoo's future traditions … but in the next instant, the throne took off again on its balloon.

'This isn't part of the plan,' said Lily to Pashmina. 'What's going on?' They squinted to see what was happening. A small airplane was towing the zeppelin and, with it, the priceless Houda. They looked at who was driving the plane—it was Strike! He had struck again and was now the most wanted thief in Bagradoo.

9

Spilled Secrets

Lily was furious with Strike. The news of the stolen Houda was splashed all over the papers, making her feel totally responsible for the fiasco. She feared that she would be ridiculed right out of the palace. She went to the King and offered to leave, but to her surprise he consoled her. 'You aren't responsible for what thieves do, Lily. You did what you thought was right. Look on the bright side—there is a very happy baby elephant reunited with his mother, thanks to you and Pashmina. And don't worry, one way or another, I'll catch that slippery Strike and bring back my elephant throne.'

Despite the King's kind words, Lily couldn't face anyone. She wanted to spend some time alone, thinking about what the previous day's events had meant. While she was touched that King Khair did not hold her responsible for the fiasco of the stolen Houda, she felt terrible that it had happened as a result of her plan. She wondered if it may be best to leave before she caused any more unintended problems. She didn't want to become a royal pain!

Lily called her mother and shared everything with her.

'You can come back the moment you want to, darling. Don't forget, we are not palace people. You are just there on a little holiday. I am so glad you have enjoyed it for the most part, but your home is here, with us.'

'I know, Mom,' said Lily, knowing her mother was probably right. But this made her feel a bit sad, because she so wished she could be that palace person and also who she was—a nature blogger and scientists' daughter from Puddleton. She wanted both.

And then there was Strike. Lily felt oddly let down by someone who she'd thought she could trust. 'I mean, he helped save Trinket, but then he totally embarrassed me by stealing the Houda in broad daylight. I gave him the benefit of the doubt after he helped find Trinket and led us to the Sea Ponypups. But now, I will never trust him again,' Lily said to her mother.

'Take some time to be by yourself,' said Lily's mom. 'Take some time to yourself, Lily. Trust me, you will feel better. And whenever you want to come home, you can, and if you don't …'

'Remember, Al's your Pal!' piped in the robot diary.

Lily managed a smile and even a little laugh, and said goodbye to her mother.

She wandered about the palace grounds wistfully, lost in her thoughts. Quill spotted her as she strolled past his den.

'You seem a bit pensive,' said Quill, sensing that she was not feeling her usual self. 'Just the right mood to lose yourself in some scientific study, I'd say. Come on now, nothing can be that bad. What do you say to a chance to look through the microscope?'

Lily's eyes widened for just a moment. An offer to see what Quill was studying was a rare opportunity, one that very few were offered.

'Really?' said Lily. 'Are you sure? You don't have to do that for me, Quill, don't worry about me.'

'I know I don't, but I'd love for you to see it. It is something I've been observing for years now, and I've really wanted to share it with somebody who can tell me what they think.'

Quill set up the large, old microscope, with its dozens of worn-out knobs and settings showing years and years of use, and lowered the glass so Lily could have a look. Lily took a deep breath as if she were about to plunge into a big ocean of possibilities, and dove right in. What came into focus were blue discs that bumped into each other, glowed for a moment and then vanished in a flash. Lily had never seen such a brilliant luminous blue before.

'What is this, Quill? And what's that scent in the room?' she asked, looking around her.

'It is blue pine,' said Quill. 'The elixir of the lone blue pine tree that stands alone in the forgotten forest range. This tree is ancient, and its pinecones glow once in a blue moon for every generation to see ... but there's more, Lily.'

'Is it a mystic boon?'

'Yes, it is, my dear. No one knows about the blue pine's magical properties. A drop of the blue elixir from a glowing pine can heal all pain. This is a secret from the Ledger that I have shared with no one. I thought you might like to learn more about it, but of course, you cannot tell anyone.'

'You trust me, Quill?' asked Lily, almost tearing up from the magic and wonder of the story, and that he had shared it with her.

'Yes, I do. We all do,' said Quill. 'We know you are a friend of the palace. If I have plotted my weather glowcast correctly, the blue pine will glow tonight. Are you ready for a hike?'

'You bet!' said Lily. 'I've never had a gloomy day turn around so quickly.'

'But Lily, there is a danger this could all go wrong. If a twisted force comes into play, the elixir will no longer soothe pain. Once swallowed, it becomes a dangerous toxin that numbs the conscience. Whoever drinks it could become a very dangerous person indeed. It was all in the Ledger.'

'Yikes,' said Lily.

'Well, not the most scientific summing up of the situation, but yes,' said Quill, 'yikes indeed.'

'So, in other words, no trying to take a sip of the elixir as an experiment,' said Lily.

'That would be a no,' said Quill, with a laugh.

Soon, Lily and Quill were bumping along in their jeep on the road up to the forgotten forest range.

'We should be there any minute now …'

And, sure enough, as they turned around the final bend, several pine trees came into view, standing in the midst of a vast meadow. The one in the front was not the great, towering thing that Lily had expected; it was a small, knobbly looking pine tree with sharp needles, grey green leaves and tiny pinecones.

The two fell into a hushed silence.

'It is remarkable, isn't it?'

'Can we go closer?' asked Lily.

'Let us give it some space. It does best alone, so we should watch it from afar, Lily. Sometimes the best thing you can do for nature is to go nowhere near.'

So, the two just watched. Lily pulled out her binoculars and drew some sketches on her tablet of what she saw through them. Quill made a note or two of what birds he saw sitting on the pine tree's branches.

And then, as they watched, they both said together, 'Is it just me … or are the pinecones starting to look blue?'

They rubbed their eyes, craned their necks and squinted as they took their binoculars out again. Gently and slowly, the sun began to set, making the pinecones glow. Lily watched in awe as the light blue glow turned brighter in the twilight sky. The whole scene—the pink and orange of the dusk, the fading green of the pine trees, the inky silhouette of the mountains and the glowing blue pines—created a view that was magical.

Lily and Quill sat in silence, taking it all in, when they were interrupted by a sudden noise. A fleet of cars arrived in a dusty cloud, one after the other. Men jumped out and started to walk in the direction of the tree. Lily looked through her binoculars.

'Who are they? Are they tourists? Should we go tell them to keep away from the tree?'

'No, that would only make them more curious. Let's see what they are up to.'

As Lily and Quill took turns to look through the binoculars, they saw the men coming closer and closer to them.

'Sightseeing hours are over. Get out of here,' one of them said, approaching Lily and Quill's jeep.

'By that logic, you should be leaving too,' said Quill in the most strong and commanding voice Lily had heard him use.

The man laughed and signalled to the others in the distance.

'Looks like Grandpa here is in the mood for a friendly fight.'

The men came closer, and it was clear now that Lily and Quill were completely outnumbered. They must act fast; there was not much time to lose.

'Oh hello, gentlemen. How nice to have like-minded people up here—nature lovers like yourself. It was starting to get dark, and we hoped we'd have some human company,' Quill said.

The men did not look like they wanted to be friendly. One of them looked Quill up and down and said, 'You look like the nature type alright. So, tell us what's so special about this tree that we had to trek all the way up here for. That too on a Sunday evening, to get a bunch of pinecones. I have a feeling it's not for Christmas decorations … Tell us, professor. I'm sure you know, otherwise you wouldn't be here, would you?'

'Oh, I'm sure I don't know,' said Quill. 'I'm quite sure I don't, in fact. I just came to admire …'

'Well, I think the fact that they glow blue—' said the muffled voice of Al the Pal. Lily was horrified. Al was being a true robot, answering questions. She pretended to cough to drown out his words, but it was too late.

'Ah, glow blue, do they? I wouldn't mind a portable night light …' the man said, turning to the tree, trying to get a closer look. 'Is that a talking phone you've got? Smarter than the professor, I'd say,' he said to Lily with a snarky laugh.

Quill and Lily wished the timing was different, but it wasn't. The lone pine tree's cones started to slowly but surely glow.

'Time for some cone picking,' said one of the men.

'Oh no, sir, the moment you pluck the cones, the light goes out,' Quill added quickly.

'That would be no good,' said one of the men.

'So what's all the fuss about? They sent us here to get the pinecones and now you say that they're of no use.'

'I think he's just messing with us ...' said a man in the back.

'Look,' said Quill, thinking it might just be best to be honest with them. 'The pinecones glow blue because the blue comes from the roots of the tree all the way up to the trunk and branches. If you remove the cone from the tree, it simply won't glow.'

'So, that blue stuff is something special, eh? Now, what it does and why it's so special we can't really say ... but there's just one way to find out. Who's going to be our volunteer?'

'Not me,' said the thin man.

'Nor me,' said a few others, laughing.

'Then how about you, professor? Either you tell us what's so special about this funny blue ...'

'Or you show us,' another man completed the sentence.

One man took Quill by the arm and walked him to the tree. Another took the cap off what looked like a dirty water bottle. He yanked at one of the pinecones that was glowing bright blue. He squeezed it until a few blue drops came out and fell into his bottle, where it sparkled a bright, iridescent blue.

He took a drop and rubbed it on his palm. Nothing happened. It simply vanished, leaving a faint glow. The man shook the bottle, sniffed it and was about to taste it when he changed his mind.

'How about a little sip for you, professor, a sip of your favourite blue champagne? A little bit never hurt anyone!' They all laughed.

All this while, Lily sat in the jeep, frozen. She had no idea what she should do. Perhaps she should sound the horn and attract attention. Hopefully this frightening situation would then be over, and she could go home. In front of her, she could see the pinecones now glowing so bright that they were truly like Christmas lights. A few drops of the blue liquid oozed out of them, collecting under the trees like little blue crystals.

'Fancy a sip of some pine wine?' laughed one of the men with a broken tooth, finding his own joke funnier than anyone else did. 'Sorry, we don't have any cheese to go with it.' More laughter echoed around them.

'Go on, take a sip, professor.'

Quill had no choice; he knew what he had to do. He only wished he had told Lily about the antidote, the universal antidote that sat in a little glass vial in his study. Now, without it, he would just have to wait for the effects of the liquid he was going to swallow to wear off. He wouldn't know right from wrong in a while—it was a risk he had to take to get these men off his back. All he had to do was try not to say anything, anything at all.

'Sure, I'll taste it, and I think I have some string cheese in my pocket. Always keep a snack handy …' said Quill, trying to alleviate their suspicions.

Quill took a sip. There was silence for a few seconds. Then, the usually quiet Quill, slowly but surely, transformed.

'So, chaps,' said Quill. 'Want to make a quick buck? Let me tell you a little something about the blue pine. This thing, if tapped, can make us all rich, very rich. This isn't your everyday glow-in-the-dark ink. A drop of this elixir will numb any pain you are feeling. Except a broken heart, of course. Whether it is headache, tired legs, back ache—you name it. A drop of this stuff, and you're all set. You'll be doing the tango in no time.'

'Now we're talking,' said a man who seemed to be the leader of the group.

'Let's juice this baby. We will sell by the thimble,' said another one of the men.

'Too bad this little Christmas tree only glows for a few more hours, and its properties only last a few seconds after it drips from the pinecone. Not quite something we can bottle for later, I'm afraid, boys …' said Quill, so very different from the Quill that Lily knew. 'But I have a great business idea. How about this …'

Lily could only watch in shock as the twisted force of the blue pine ran its course, with Quill as the guinea pig. He had, very truly, totally lost his conscience!

Quill continued, 'We line up a bunch of grandmas with back aches. You must tell them to get over here real quick for a thimble of this stuff. I am sure they will cough up a lot of dosh for a sound night's sleep. So, what do you think?' he said, with the flourish of someone who had just pitched the brightest business idea.

'Does not sound like the best business plan, my man. By the time we get a bunch of geriatrics on a bus here at least two hours would've passed, and it will be morning. When will this thing glow next, tomorrow night?'

'Oh, not for another eighty-nine years, to be exact,' said Quill as helpfully as possible. 'Put that in the calendar I say, and plan on getting your kids very rich that day.'

'What an idiot,' said the leader.

'Got to give him a prize for having the worst nose for business ever!' said his lackey.

They started laughing at Quill, and Lily thought all of it was over until one of the men looked at him curiously.

'You told us nothing earlier, and now you are spilling the tea? Something's up. All this after you drank a sip of the blue juice …'

'Of course, smarty pants,' said Quill. 'You know what else the elixir does? To those who touch it, it is a balm for pain. But to those who drink it …'

Lily listened with her eyes shut tight—Quill was about to spill the secret of the twisted force written in the Ledger!

'It makes you lose your conscience. You don't know right from wrong; you'll do anything you like to make a quick buck. So, what say, shall we make a quick buck together? Looks like you all lost your conscience without even needing to drink any of this.'

The men were listening in amazement, not sure how to respond, when Quill proceeded with, 'Want more secrets of the Ledg—'

Before he could finish his sentence, there came a loud "Caaaaawww" from overhead. "Caww cawww caww."

'The sound of a crow,' said Al. 'Or is that a secret too?'

It was Kaw, Strike's crow. It circled around the tree noisily and perched itself on Lily's jeep window, dropping a little note into her hands:

'Give this antidote to Quill,
So he doesn't do a bigger spill.'

And then, Kaw proceeded to create chaos, cawing loudly and flapping all around the men, who tried their best to shoo it away, only to see the noisy crow come back.

In the chaos, Lily knew she had her chance. She walked up to Quill and gave him a few drops of the antidote. Within moments, Quill became a bit more like himself.

'You were saying something about a ledge? A ledge? A shelf? Spill it, Grandpa …'

'Oh, nothing at all,' said Quill. 'Nothing at all, just an old man blathering.'

'Oh, what a grand waste of time.'

'The old fool really is an old fool.'

'And he wants to do business with us! Ha ha, no thanks … a bus of old people, what a great business plan.'

'See you in another eighty-nine years.'

'I'm going home,' announced one of the men, and they all drove off in the dust cloud they had come in.

'I am so sorry, Lily,' said a very shaken Quill. 'So very sorry to have scared you so. Thank you for that antidote. Did Kaw the crow bring it? I tell you, that Strike and his crow, you never know whether to love them or hate them. One day they get up to terrible mischief and the next day they help you out when you're in trouble. Yes, that's Strike for you. Always a mystery. But I'm glad he hasn't yet been caught because today he certainly came to my rescue. When we get back, I will tell the King that there are people who seem to know more than they should, and there is trouble ahead. But before that I must first thank you for being there to help me.'

```
Hi, friends of the Glog. Today we went to a
beautiful pine range …
```

Lily shut off her camera.

'Al,' she said, 'it's kind of hard to Glog without telling people anything … what do I do? I mean, I want to share so much but I can't compromise the secrets of the island.'

'Good point,' said Al. 'How about focusing on the palace interiors? People love that stuff too.'

'The nature and palace interiors blog … hmmm, doesn't quite have the same ring to it as the Glog, does it …' said Lily, and they both laughed.

'You can laugh?' said Lily, realizing she was laughing with a robot.

'I didn't know I could, either,' said Al.

10

Vintage Mean Girls

'Lily,' said the King on the intercom to her first thing in the morning. 'If you're not too busy today, we wouldn't mind your help with something. The Dowager Queen is having a tea party today, and it looks like your elephant friend might have created a crack in her plans. I'd be most grateful if you could help.'

Lily had only ever heard about the Dowager Queen, who was King Khair's mother. The thought of meeting the grand old lady made Lily feel quite nervous. But she had been summoned, so off she went to the Dowager's quarters.

In her visiting room, the Dowager was seated on a low chaise, her silhouette regal. She was poised and aristocratic from top to bottom; her low bun looked elegant, and her long cane rested gracefully at her side. The room smelled like fresh flowers and a hint of cake. But as Lily walked in, she could tell that the lady was not in the best of moods. *Gulp.* The Dowager turned slowly in Lily's direction, not quite acknowledging Lily, but getting straight to the point.

'As they say in America, everyone here is fresh out of ideas on how I should throw a tea party for my friends. All thanks to a baby elephant that ran amok, crushing every set of porcelain I own.' The Dowager clearly did not believe in wasting time in idle chit-chat.

'That would be Parumm,' said Lily.

'Pa—who?'

'Parumm, Your Highness. The baby elephant? He's gone now. He's back with his mom.'

'But not before shattering all my bone china. There is not one set that isn't broken, not one.'

Lily had no idea how to react, and what came out next was probably the last thing she wanted to say. 'Great excuse to go shopping then, right?'

'That joke was "cringe",' said Al the Pal in whisper mode. 'I have a joke button for when you need it. You do know that, right, Lily?'

Lily winced. She knew Al was right. The Dowager looked up at Lily for the first time and gave her what one would best describe as a withering look.

'The ladies I am inviting can't be asked to sip tea out of store-bought china.'

'Oh, I am sorry—I didn't know that,' muttered Lily.

'I heard you helped with Pashmina's fashion shoot when things did not go according to plan. The *Royal High Tea* magazine are all set for a photo shoot, not to mention my school girlfriends, to whom invitations have already been sent,' said the Dowager, pointing with her cane at a trolley stacked with the broken cups, saucers, tea pots and sugar bowls. 'I suggest you find a way to salvage the tea party. My classmates back in the day were what, in today's parlance, are called "mean girls". They were mean then and are not easy to impress even now. But this time, I had hoped to knock their socks off, and if I can't do that I may just have to cancel the tea.'

'Oh, that won't be necessary. I'm sure we can come up with something real quick,' said Lily.

'The King and Pashmina seem to think you are creative, good with ideas. I'm still waiting to hear even one.'

Lily totally missed the reprimand and was so flattered by her new reputation that she started to blush.

'Oh, thanks, Dowager Queen—that's a really sweet compliment.'

'Well, do get on with it then, as they say,' said the Dowager, elegantly lifting herself up with a little help from the cane, and starting to glide away in aristocratic strides.

Lily took out bits of china from the trolley, piece by piece. She could not find a single set that was not chipped or cracked.

'How about a mix and match tea party?' she said, just before the Dowager left the room.

'A what and what party?'

'A mix and match tea party, where we use items from different tea sets to create a new set. But with another twist …'

'This sounds like enough of a twist to me,' said the Dowager who, despite trying to look as uninterested as possible, wasn't quite able to conceal her curiosity.

'It's just an idea I had,' said Lily. 'And I hope I can make it work.'

'Well, I sure hope so too,' said the Dowager, before walking away in a swish of skirt and cane.

Lily bowed quickly and awkwardly as the Dowager left and immediately phoned Quill.

'Quill, I am going to need some fast-drying waterproof glue that is food grade,' declared Lily.

'Good morning to you too, Lily. Nice sunny day, isn't it? Or have you no time for pleasantries?' said Quill.

'I need to fix something—The Dowager Queen's orders.'

'Oh, the DQ—well now, that is a whole new level of urgent,' said Quill.

'Please help me, Quill. I need something that sticks, dries instantly and is waterproof and food grade,' said Lily, in a mad hurry. 'The Dowager Queen is not exactly happy after Parumm crushed her bone china. She is having a tea party, and we need to fix her tea set. So yes, the glue also has to be totally transparent.'

'Ah, I see. Your tall order just got taller, but I think I have just the thing for you.'

'What's that?'

'It is moss sap. It's gooey green when wet and totally invisible when dry. And, as it happens, it is food grade. You could mould a cup out of it, let it dry and drink from that cup.'

'And how much time does it take to dry?'

'Ten seconds after you squeeze it from the plant.'

'Is it a magical gift of nature?'

'No, but it should be. It's a magical last-minute fix for anything that is broken. Everything but …'

'A broken heart!' they said in unison, laughing.

'Okay, so let's go get it. I haven't much time …' said Lily gratefully. 'The Dowager wants it done now, tap tap,' Lily imitated the Dowager's signature cane tap.

'For that, Lily, you're going to have to go to the fountain courtyard and collect the moss from the old wall there. It is soft and spongy to the touch and stands apart from the other moss by being the brightest green, almost neon. Bring the moss back here and squeeze it into a beaker that I will keep warm for you, so that it doesn't set. Use it like hot glue to fix your china and it will set permanently in ten seconds. This will make it even stronger than before.'

Lily found her way into the fountain courtyard that looked like a magical universe with beautiful marble urns and sculptures, the sound of water and rainbows dancing everywhere as the sunlight caught the water. Lily started to hum a little tune her mother had always sung to her as a child. As she sat there, humming and gazing at her own reflection in the fountain water, Lily wondered how she could feel so at home in this far-away island kingdom.

Just then, someone else's reflection appeared in the water next to her. It was the Dowager. 'This is one of my favourite places in the palace,' said the Dowager. 'And that song happens to be a favourite of mine too. I'm surprised you know it so well. You certainly are a curious little one.'

Lily was surprised to see the Dowager there, looking at her with such warmth. The two just sat there for a bit and shared the moment, the light, the sound of the fountain. For once, Lily didn't feel the need to say anything at all. All of a sudden, she was missing home, especially her mother.

'You're unusually quiet,' said the Dowager.

Lily smiled. 'I suppose I'm missing my mom.'

'You were brave to come all this way,' said the Dowager. 'Why did you choose Bagradoo?'

'My parents are geneticists, and my genetic test revealed that I have a bit of Bagradoo in me.'

'Well, I can tell you that whatever runs in your blood is never as big as what runs in your heart … and you certainly seem to have Bagradoo in your heart,' said the Dowager, before elegantly moving away.

Lily gathered some moss from the old wall and carefully brought it into Quill's den, where she donned her visor and set to work squeezing the moss sap and setting it to boil in a warm beaker. The bubbling liquid soon thickened to a glue.

'What if we don't just fix the pieces but mix them too?' said Lily to Al the Pal.

'You mean mix and mismatch?' said Al the Pal.

'I thought a mix-and-match party was unusual enough for me,' said a voice at the door. 'But it won't hurt to try.'

To Lily's amazement, the Dowager came in and even offered to lend a hand. Together, they tinkered with the tea sets, squeezing little drops of the fast-setting glue onto the chipped china. They got creative and mixed handles and spouts to create a wild new set that was truly one of a kind.

'I am sure your guests can't criticize you now,' said Lily to the Dowager.

'Oh, mean girls will be mean girls,' she said. 'But I think in creativity, I might just have one-upped them this time with your help.'

'Well, I don't know much about outright meanness, but I do know a thing or two about what it feels like to be ignored at school,' said Lily. 'That feeling of not being cool enough, of having to prove yourself, just never goes away.'

'And it might never. Look at me. I am the Dowager Queen and I am desperately sticking bits of broken china together.'

The two had a hearty laugh.

The mean girls soon arrived for tea. They chatted and oohed and aahed and photographed themselves with the wild new tea set as if it was the newest rage in town. The Dowager enjoyed herself too, occasionally pausing to sit back and watch her guests enjoying the eccentric decorations, delicious cakes and savoury treats.

'How do you think it went?' Lily asked when it was over.

'Well, I'd say it was a smashing success!' remarked Al the Pal enthusiastically.

The Dowager looked amused at the strange talking diary and burst into laughter!

11

Fresh Out of Water

It was one of those days that made no sense until suddenly, it all made sense and nothing was the same again. So, here's what happened. I was back in my own room, and was awoken by a crazy loud rattling on my windowpane. I had no idea what on earth it could be. It turned out to be a bird, not an angry bird but a crazy bird, totally cuckoo. Well, not quite a cuckoo, but a crow. You can probably guess who the crow was—it was Kaw.

Hmmmm. It belongs to Strike, of course. I couldn't trust Strike, so I didn't want to trust Kaw. But then, poor crow. Maybe it was in distress because Strike was nowhere around. So, I opened the window, and Kaw flew right in. It flapped its wings madly and flew away, as if it wanted me to follow it. How do I know he wanted me to follow? Well, if you've had a puppy who wants you to follow him, you know what that looks like. This was not very different.

Before following Kaw, I popped into the bathroom to freshen up. I turned on the faucet—there was no water. I tried the bath—again, no water. In the end, I had to make do with water from the jug. I washed my face and brushed my teeth. Then, I followed Kaw.

As it happened, it had called Quill as well, and we both followed the crow, you know, as you do. Quill started muttering something about there not being any water in his room, and when he realized the same thing had happened in my room, he did a little inspection. We went past the fountain courtyard, no water. Strange. The garden sprinklers were dry too.

'I don't think it's a case of old-fashioned palace plumbing. Looks like the water in the island has, all but truly, run out.'

We soon reached the foot of a tall mountain, where Kaw stopped and did this funny crow hover, looking quite clumsy. It sure was effective, though, because it was impossible to ignore its flapping, circling and cawing.

'I don't speak crow, but I think it wants us to climb,' Al the Pal said. Yes, by now I pretty much brought him everywhere with me.

'Climb the peak? But it's the home of the Crystal Geyser.' Quill's voice took on a hushed and respectful tone. When he saw the puzzled look on my face, he went on.

'The Crystal Geyser is Bagradoo's fountain of water. It is an aquifer, an underground spring with the purest water known to mankind. And everyone assumes that, come what may, this water will remain in endless supply. The crystal-clear purity of the water is preserved by the fact that no one can come near the source. No one but the keeper of the waters, an old lady who lives in a hut on the mountain.'

'Sounds like a top-notch security arrangement,' said Al. 'Please tell me he's joking. The island's precious water source protected by a senior citizen in a hut?'

Kaw's cawing got more frantic. 'It looks like we need to go have a look. And it's not going to be easy, not with my knees.'

And my fear of heights, I wanted to add, but I said nothing and off we went, one step at a time, to reach the untouched crystal peak. The climb was beautiful but tough. Once, Quill seemed to lose his grip on the rock and I gave him my hand, only to lose my grip too. We were just about to take a serious double tumble when, as if by a miracle, something hooked my backpack. I thought maybe it was the branch of a tree, but no, it was a proper hook-on stick. Right above me was a familiar-looking figure rappelling down the mountain. He had caught our fall by hooking my backpack to a long stick. One look at that funny hat and there was no mistaking

Strike. Of course, it would be him. With Kaw overhead, could Strike be far behind?

'Thanks, young man. I fear I would have taken young Lily down with me. So, it was you who asked the crow to fetch us, is that right?'

'Yes, Sir,' said Strike, tipping his hat politely at Quill.

'Things certainly seem to have gotten unusually busy on the hill.'

'Would you like some water?' asked Strike. With a mischievous smile, he offered us a plastic water bottle with a sticker on it that said "Crystal Shyne". 'It's the same water we drink for free, but they are bottling and selling it to us for quite a profit …' he added with a wink.

Quill couldn't believe what he was hearing. 'Who is doing what?'

We picked up pace, and Quill seemed to no longer worry about his knee. He was so keen to get to the top that he scrambled, slid and did whatever he needed to keep up with Strike. As thirsty as he got, he refused even a sip of the bottled water and only drank from the little springs that flowed down the mountainside. I did the same out of respect for his eccentricity and for the geyser.

We soon reached close to the top. Where I was expecting to see a clear, tranquil lake with nothing but the blue sky and clouds above it, I instead saw something altogether different. There was a whole assembly line of tanks and pumps—the crystal peak had turned into a factory for Crystal Shyne!

'How could they possibly get all this up here when it is so hard to climb the mountain?' I asked.

The answer presented itself. We saw a helicopter make its wobbly landing. Below it, someone's hat was sent flying—it was Lady Devi's. She was seated on a folding chair, overseeing the business. Standing beside her was Sir Vipin, giving his orders like a music conductor. When Lady Devi's hat blew off with the helicopter's breeze, she had just been about to scowl, but she realized the chopper was actually doing her coffee run. The door opened, and her butler stepped out, carrying her famous green coffee smoothie, complete with a straw, all carefully balanced on an oval silver tray. These were brought to her as her pillows were plumped, a footrest arranged and a giant screen placed in front of her, playing her daytime soap opera, which she watched with a giant headset to keep the background noise out.

'Where on earth is the keeper of the Crystal Geyser while this preposterous nonsense is going on? She used to be right there.' When Quill looked through his binoculars, he almost lost his balance. What had once been a thatched bamboo hut was now something else altogether—a pink villa with a meandering swimming pool that had giant swan floats, a jacuzzi and a mini golf course.

'Oh, what a travesty. No one is supposed to set foot on this peak but now, it has become a circus. How did the keeper of the Geyser agree to this? Did they bribe her? She hates people, she hates disturbance and she hates any noise except the sound of water, which is why she wanted the job and has had it for forty years. What happened? How could she have had such a sudden change of heart? How could she allow helicopters and builders here? Such a sudden loss of conscience …'

'Quill, did you say she lost her conscience? In that case there can only be one explanation, right? Yes, I think it has to be the blue pine.'

'So then, the Ledger has truly been leaked, hasn't it, Lily?'

'Yes, Quill,' I said, feeling awful for him. This was the last thing he wanted.

'They certainly chose the right person to give it to. They didn't have enough to turn the whole island into a bunch of conscienceless minions, but they had enough to manipulate an old curmudgeon to make their fortunes with Crystal Shyne. Our island is in danger, Lily. We need to tell the King at once. If one twisted force has come into play, it's just a matter of time before the others …'

I took pictures of the whole scene as quickly as possible. Strike was patiently waiting for us at a distance. 'Probably a good idea to go tell the King that the Island Minister has his own plans for Bagradoo,' he called. 'Kaw and I have, of course, known all along, but who would believe a thief?'

'Yes, why would they?' said Lily. 'You won back my trust by helping us with Trinket, only to break it by stealing the Houda!'

'Oh, that was just a friendly robbery. I've always had a long-standing, friendly wager with the King. I like a bit of drama and public spectacle, and I've a reputation to uphold as the most-wanted thief. Don't worry, I'll return the Houda soon enough. It is the royal family's heirloom after all. But the water here belongs to all of us and they want to sell it back at a profit to the people of the island. Now, that's something I'll never do,' Strike said, as he helped us carefully make our way back down the mountain.

Back at the palace, Quill went straight to the King, while I went to tell Pashmina that the island may just be out of water real soon, and the person responsible seemed to be the Island Minister himself. How was I to explain this to a princess in the middle of her gown fittings?

I tried to knock on Pashmina's door as confidently as possible. An assistant opened it and gave the kind of frozen smile that said, 'Who do you think you are, disturbing the Princess in the middle of her dress fitting?'

'I'm so sorry to disturb her, but there is a matter I need to speak to her about, and it really is quite pressing.'

'The Princess has on a dress with thirty-seven pins placed in precision—also a bit pressing. Come back in three hours.'

I could tell he was in no mood to help; I had no choice.

'PASHMINAAA!' I yelled through the crack in the door.

Pashmina gave a start and whirled around. This made the pins in her dress start to

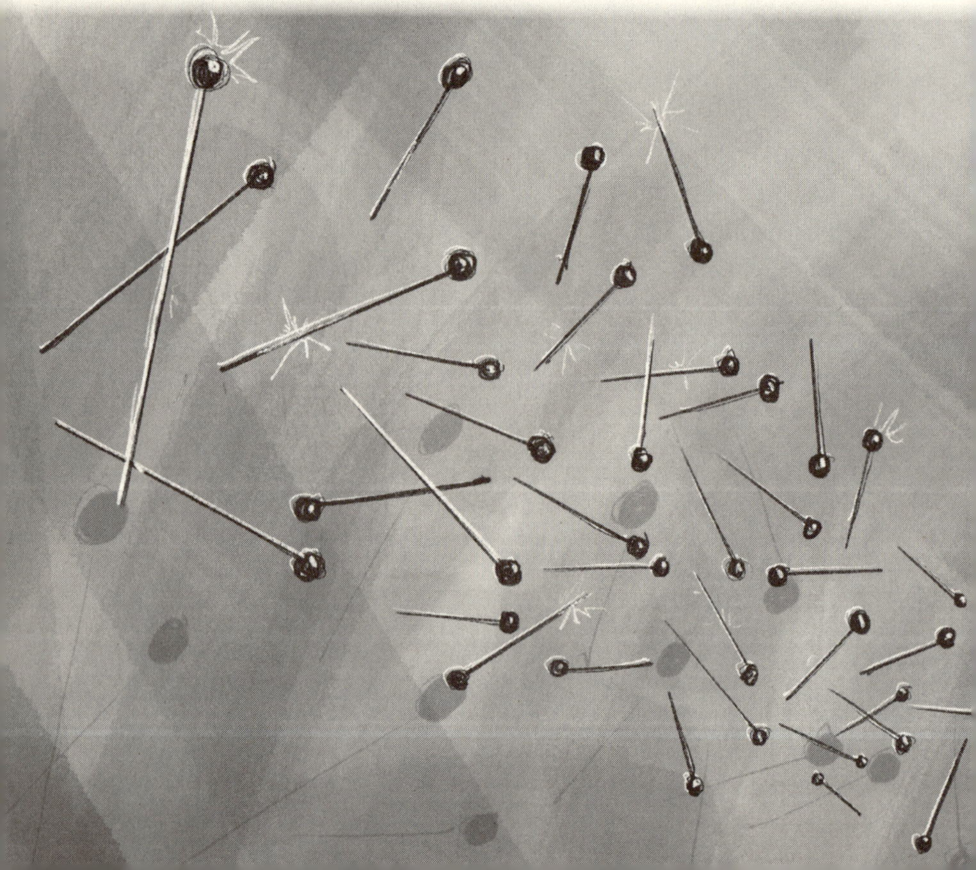

pop, one after the other. All thirty-seven of them flew up in the air and landed on the floor, in what could only be called a pin-drop silence. As the pins flew, I saw the faces of the dressmakers go in dramatic slow motion from serious to shocked to horrified.

I felt terrible, but there was nothing I could do. I had to have Pashmina's attention. Hopefully, she would understand me later.

'What is it, Lily … what's so urgent?'

Once I'd told her the news, she said, 'Let's tell Daddy, he needs to know. There will be no water for the party. Maybe we can just buy out that Crystal Shyne, just this once, and take care of it later.'

While it might not have been the reaction we were hoping for, fortunately, Pashmina was going to help us explain to the King that his most trusted Island Minister and his cousin were up to something dangerous at the crystal peak.

In the King's chamber, the conversation was already well underway.

'So, you say that there were people bottling water from the Crystal Geyser? And you say that those people were Sir Vipin and Lady Devi?'

'Yes, Your Majesty,' said Quill, 'I am afraid so. And I had to check, to make sure they were not doing this with your knowledge.'

'This is the first I'm hearing of it.'

'If that is the case, Your Majesty, then this is a big problem,' said Quill. 'The

Crystal Geyser must never go dry because then Bagradoo will lose its only source of fresh water forever,' continued Quill, tearfully.

'Let's not get carried away, Quill, but we'll send some people to inspect things up there at once. We must find out what Vipin and Lady Devi are up to. I have trusted them for years and will not believe a word against them without proof. For all you know, there may be a perfectly reasonable explanation. But meanwhile, the ball must go on … Tomorrow, Pashmina will be crowned with the Opal Tiara. We must waste no time. In light of all that we know, her place as my heir should be clear. Crystal clear, should I say, so that she can come into her responsibilities that only seem to be growing day by day. For soon, the Opal Throne will be hers, the first woman in a long line of men. She will make her late mother and me proud.'

So, that's what I have to report to you today, my friends of the Glog. It has been one crazy day, and I'm sure there is more in store tomorrow.

The only problem is that I'm not allowed to share this with you because, as Quill said, everything in the Ledger stays in the Ledger. I wish I could share this with you, but for now, it must stay in my diary. For me and me alone. But you sure helped me get it off my chest.

And then, Lily pressed delete. She was a trusted insider at the palace and had to prioritize that over her Glog.

Later, as Lady Devi sat sipping her tea in her parlour, and Sir Vipin stood nervously, talking on both his phones, DJ walked into the room.

'Why the serious face, Mother? You have been in such good form lately. What happened?'

'Well, another one of our business ventures is ruined,' said Lady Devi. 'Someone decided to come snooping around at the crystal peak and when they saw us bottling Crystal Shyne, they said it was royal orders that all unauthorized work stop at once because of the Princess's debutante ball tomorrow. And when they asked me what we were doing up there, I told them I thought it would be a nice gift for the Princess—a shiny new brand of bottled water. What a ridiculous idea, but you must credit me for it, right Vipin?'

'Certainly, my lady, certainly. That was some presence of mind. Of course, we had no such plan. And if we had not been stopped, can you just imagine the heights our business would have reached? We would've marketed our own water around the world as beauty in a glass, health in a bottle, glow in a can. And as for our islanders, we would've started selling water to them even though, all this while, they had been getting it for free. I mean, how could no one think of this before? It's about appreciating what you've got. One never does so until one pays full price for it, or more.'

Lady Devi said, 'Really, the King should have hired me as his financial consultant, but he never did. Someone needs to have ideas around here, yes, Vipin?'

'Oh yes, my lady, of course. It was all you. And just imagine, after him there will be Pashmina!' said Sir Vipin, rolling his eyes.

'Surely, you can do better than be a dressmaker to that heir-head,' said Lady Devi, turning to DJ. 'You should be the one on the throne, young man. With a bit of ambition and the right manoeuvres, why, I would have been there years ago if I were you. If only you had more ambition for yourself than your—what do you call it—atelier.'

'Well, it was Lily who advised me to do it, and I didn't think it would hurt.'

'Oh, that ridiculous tourist is such a nuisance. Who does she think she is, telling you, a royal prince, what you should be doing?' said Lady Devi.

'Well, she also told us that she was the one who went up to the mountain and saw the bottling of Crystal Shyne.'

'What?'

'Yes, Mother,' DJ said with some hesitation. 'I was supervising Pashmina's dress fitting when Lily walked in and told her that she and Quill saw unusual activity up at the crystal peak.'

'So, it was she who snooped on us? She? That nosey photographer was always trouble.' Lady Devi worked herself into a rage that got her out of her chair. 'We have had just enough of that meddlesome outsider. It is time we got rid of her. It is time we took the throne. Our time is now! And we will win at all costs.'

There was a tremor in the room as Lady Devi became increasingly more furious and calm, in turns. Meanwhile, Sir

Vipin went very quiet, knowing the only way to handle the storm was to let it pass. After this, he knew, another very big one was coming.

As for DJ, one would have no idea what he was thinking.

12

Tiara Farewell

Plans were in full swing for Pashmina's grand ball. There was more to be done than ever before at the palace.

Chef Khan was in full form, directing his many assistants as they prepared a monstrous amount of food for the entire island to feast on.

Pashmina was visibly excited—no longer the nonchalant Princess. This was the moment she wasn't sure she was ready for, but she knew she had to rise to it.

One evening, as Lily, Pashmina, Quill, Sir Vipin and the King sat in the palace drawing room, Pashmina turned to Lily. 'I want to say thank you,' she said.

'To me?' said Lily, looking behind her as if Pashmina was talking to someone else.

'Yes, of course, to you, Lily,' she said with a smile, warmly squeezing Lily's hand. 'Thank you for making me fall in love with my own home again. I had taken it all for granted. And now, I know there's no place like Bagradoo.'

Lily was about to react when a palace guard came running in, unannounced.

'Sir, Sir, there is a problem. The Opal in the Princess's tiara—'

'Yes? What about the Opal in the tiara?' said the King, his voice as composed as the guard's was stressed.

'It's gone missing.'

A hushed gasp rippled through the room. All eyes were on the King for his reaction.

Quill's face became ashen. 'Your highness … the Opal …' he stuttered. 'It is the island's most salient gift of nature! And as you know, our island without the safeguard of the Opal … could well and truly be doomed.'

'I hear you, dear Quill,' said the King quite firmly. 'But there is no reason to assume the worst before learning the facts.'

'I know, Sir, but the Opal's tw-tw-tw-twisted force …' Quill found it so hard to say those words, he whispered them, 'If the Opal's twisted force comes into play, I would have no idea how to control it. All these years, I have failed to crack the code that holds the secret cure.' Having said this, Quill sank into his chair and started to mutter softly to himself. Lily went over and put a gentle hand on his shoulder to comfort him.

'Quill,' said King Khair, 'we all share your concern for the Opal. After all, the Opal presides over all celebrations at Bagradoo—we can't possibly host Pashmina's ball without it.'

'Vipin!' said the King to the Island Minister, who had been unusually quiet. 'We need our best search team on the job right away. The Opal has only been gone a few hours and our men and women will retrieve it. I want everyone in the palace to stay where they are. No one can leave the palace, or even the room they are in. Everyone but the search team remain exactly where they are at this moment. Have the team search every corner of our island for the Opal. It has not left the palace in hundreds of years and is not going to leave today.'

'Yes, Your Majesty, right away, Your Majesty,' said Sir Vipin, who went on to immediately set the protocol in action.

But before he left the room, the King said, 'Just one thing, Vipin. Are you part of the search team?'

'No sir, I give them instructions.'

'In that case, you too would be required to remain here.'

'Yes, Your Majesty,' said Vipin, going pale for a second before regaining his cool composure.

'And one more little thing, Vipin. What exactly is going on at the Crystal Geyser? I am sure there is a perfectly sensible explanation as you are in charge of island matters. Since you were seen there, I wondered if there is something I need to know.'

'Oh, if I may,' said Lady Devi, all flowers and perfume in her voice. No one knew when she had entered the glass ballroom, but she had. 'It was to be my surprise present for Pashmina's big day. A trendy line of flavoured water is all the rage with young people these days, and you know how popular Pashmina is. I thought it would be a great little gift for her—her own line of bottled water. That's what the factory is for.'

'Perhaps we all need to brush up on the island's rules,' said the King to Sir Vipin. 'Any child on the island would tell you that it is forbidden to meddle with our source of water—even to go there without a royal decree. Only the keeper of the water is permitted on the peak. A factory! That cannot be allowed, not even for the Princess.'

'We had assumed that in the name of the … I mean, for the sake of our wonderful Princess, exceptions could be made,' said Sir Vipin.

'We are disappointed, of course, that Pashmina can't have the present we took so long to arrange for her, but we'll obey your orders, Your Majesty, of course we will,' said Lady Devi.

'Pashmina is part of a long line of rulers who put the island first. Your idea of a line of flavoured water was thoughtful, I am sure, but one the island certainly cannot support. Let's say no more on the subject and get on with our search for the Opal.'

A search party went room by room, scouring every corner of the palace. Lily approached the King. 'Can I help with the search?'

'Best we all stay in one place and let the team do their job,' said King Khair. 'We want to get this done as efficiently as possible.'

Time went by, and everyone sat in an awkward silence.

'I think this is a good time for all the young people present here, and the old ones too, to brush up on why the Opal matters so much to Bagradoo,' the King suggested.

'Yes, Your Majesty,' said Quill, calming down instantly as he took on his professorial role. 'The Opal, as you know, my dear Bagradaens, does not always sit on the crown or the tiara. It is only ever placed there during ceremonies, in a special case that is designed for it. This is because, as you would have read in your history books, the Bagradoo Opal must never see the light of day. Because if a ray of daylight were to fall on the Opal, it will start to go from a clear luminescent to cloudy. A cloudy Opal would trigger the clouds in the sky, causing them to brew a storm over our island and then start an unstoppable rain.

'This is the mysterious power of the Opal, which is why it sits in a casket, cased in a box, behind three layers of black velvet curtain, all in an underground vault below the glass ballroom where no one can enter. Yet, we seek the power of the Opal for any big event and so a careful protocol is followed.

'The Opal's casket is removed from the hollowed chamber. It is brought up to the glass ballroom and placed in a thick cloak of velvet in a perfectly timed journey. Inside the shroud, the Opal is placed on the tiara or crown for the ceremony. The Princess, in this case, would be seated ready right beside it. The tiara with the Opal on it will be removed from the shroud and placed on her head for precisely twelve seconds. Twelve seconds, in which there will be just enough light to awaken the Opal, whose glow will illuminate the tiara and bless the Princess for twelve years. The Opal will then swiftly be cloaked and once more returned to its safe cocoon in the vault.'

When Quill concluded his explanation, the King said, 'We have no idea who broke this non-negotiable protocol at grave risk to the island.'

'What happens if this chain of events is broken? What exactly happens if the Opal sees the light of day for more than twelve seconds?' asked Lily.

'The Opal, my dear, is one of the island's strongest mystic boons that is energized by light. When it meets a ray of light, it produces a powerful energy that radiates into anyone who touches it. But sunlight for any more than a few seconds means that the clear Opal will start to turn cloudy, triggering a tempest around it. It has been known to happen, and when it did, it set off an endless rain. The rain will not calm down unless we use a counter spell. What that counter spell is, we don't know, because it is written in code in the Ledger. A code that even I have not been able to crack,' said Quill, proceeding to mutter to himself again at the worrisome thought.

'It is an ancestral memory we have,' said King Khair, regarding the last time the Opal had caused an endless rain. 'It is not a chapter we ever want to revisit. Anyway, that's a lot of information. Don't worry, I am sure the Opal will turn up. Maybe it is that Strike … but he knows better than to tinker with it. No Bagradaen ever would.'

'I wonder, I wonder who this could be …' said Quill, now thinking out loud.

'Our search party will get to the bottom of it,' said the King. 'Leave that to them.'

At that moment, the head of the search party stormed in. 'Sir, we found this, Sir …'

'You've found the Opal?! That was quick!' said the King.

But the officer held in his hand something that everyone had, for a moment, forgotten was missing. It was a large, weather-beaten old leather book that looked like it held the knowledge of many ages—the Ledger of Boons.

'Oh, by the sun, moon and stars, I shall never let you out of my sight again …' said Quill, as if reunited with a long-lost child.

'There it is,' said the King. 'I knew it was just missing, lost somewhere in the wise eclectic mess of your den.'

'Sir, I'm afraid it was not found in the den,' said the head of the search party.

'I see, well then, where was it?' asked the King.

'It was, erm, in the guest suite, Your Majesty,' he blurted out awkwardly.

'The guest suite? Which one? There are twenty-three in the palace!'

'It was found under the mattress in room number three, allotted to Miss Lily Ray,' he said, trying to sound as professional and matter-of-fact as possible.

There was silence for a moment, after which everyone turned to look at Lily. Her heart pounded so loud she could hear it. It felt as if her whole world was spinning. She looked at everybody and noticed the way their expressions had changed as they looked at her. Their eyes were turning cold, their expressions hardening, the assumptions of friendship and trust vanishing.

'Lily …?' Quill was the first to speak, slowly shaking his head. Was he shaking it in disbelief because he did not believe the man's words? Or was he shaking it in disappointment at Lily?

Lily had never felt more alone and more mortified than she did in that moment with all the eyes in the glass ballroom on her.

'Are you sure …?' said the King. 'Are you really quite sure …?'

'Yes, Sir, it was in her room alright, I saw it there myself. However—'

'Well … I hate to say this, but it is no coincidence, Your Majesty, that things really haven't been the same since we had this new visitor, have they?' Lady Devi chimed in before anybody could say anything further. 'Something or the other always seems to be going wrong. I knew this Lily was trouble, but I just didn't know how to tell you …'

Unable to bear it anymore, Lily ran out of the room. She ran hard and long without looking back—out of the ballroom and down the endless corridors back to her room, the scene of the "crime". She did not stop until she flung open her bedroom door and threw herself on her bed. She wanted badly to sob, but the sobs wouldn't come. She wished they would; instead, her mind whirred with thoughts ...

How could the Ledger be in my room? How? Could I have stolen it in my sleep? Do I sleepwalk? I'm going to ring Mom and ask if it is possible that I do things in my sleep. I just don't trust myself anymore. It's like that quilt—I thought it appeared out of nowhere and I had no memory of packing it.

At that point, Lily was willing to believe everyone but herself. She tried her mother once, twice, three times on the phone.

'Wake up, Mom, wake up ... I know it's the dead of the night for you, but please wake up.'

There was no answer.

'Sleep walking is a sign of ...' started Al the Pal, which was lying on her desk and seemed to have heard her speaking to herself.

'Not now, Al, I'm just not in the mood,' said Lily.

'Need a mood-lift, then? I got the joke for the day, want to hear it? You're it.'

'Not funny, Al, not funny,' said Lily.

'Yes, not my best, but this did seem like an emergency so I pulled out what I could.'

The little joke at her expense made Lily quite angry. She sat up, pulled out her empty backpack from under her bed and started to pack. She opened the closet and pulled out her clothes and shoes, stuffing them inside her backpack. First the gumboots she had not yet had a chance to wear, then the new clothes that DJ had helped her style. She pulled them out and looked at them. She laid them on the bed, then she decided she couldn't take them with her.

A tear rolled down Lily's cheek. She moved to her desk, sifting through her newly acquired keepsakes: a pine needle, pressed jasmine flowers. Then when she saw the picture of her parents on her desk, Lily broke down completely.

She started talking to her mother's picture. 'They think I took it, Mom, they think I took it. How could it be in my room? Did someone else put it here? When? How?'

'Happy to help,' said Al. 'Want a rundown of your day? Well, would've been nice if you took me with you but lately, you've been rather busy. And for the past twelve hours, you've been away, outside my working radius. As I've been here in the room and you didn't take me with you—'

'Okay Al, I know I've been busy. I've been busy helping at the island, you know.'

'—and as per my movement detectors, you did not enter the room except once, to put something under the mattress.'

'Huh?' said Lily. 'Al, you too are saying that I did it?'

'Oh, wait a minute,' said Al. 'Ha ha, my bad … per the biometrics of the camera, that person is not you.'

'What? Are you joking? What person?'

'The person who walked into your room this evening and put something under the mattress.'

Lily grabbed the digital diary and peered at Al the Pal's built-in closed-circuit camera, which automatically recorded the environs it was in, a sort of perennial recorded live. She looked at the footage. It was grainy but clear enough to see that someone had walked into her room. They had a large book in their hands. The person paused for a bit and looked around. Then, they bent down, lifted her mattress and placed the book under it. Lily looked as closely as she could to see who it was … it was DJ!

DJ! Her friend. The person who she had helped, the person who had helped her. Helpless DJ was not so helpless after all. What was he doing? And why? She was furious. A part of her was convinced she had to let everyone know. Yet, a part of her hesitated to reveal his crime.

'What do I do?' Lily thought out loud.

'Do … what you have to do,' said Al.

'Very helpful, Al, very helpful. Actually, that *was* very helpful. Thank you,' said Lily.

Lily ran back to the grand glass ballroom just as fast as she had left. Everyone still seemed to be there, talking in whispers. Only, there were more people in the room now, the Dowager Queen included.

'I didn't do it,' Lily said immediately as she entered.

'Nice try,' said Lady Devi.

'I didn't, and I know who did. It is all recorded here.'

'Recorded where, Lily?' asked the King.

'Here … with Al the Pal.'

'Hah, that sounds very credible,' mocked Lady Devi.

'Someone is a bit of a secret spy, it seems, huh? An undercover agent, are we! That explains all your snooping around …' said Sir Vipin, his voice thick with sarcasm.

The contents of Lily's camera were projected on a big screen. There, in plain sight, was DJ, walking into Lily's room with something large under his arm, putting it under her mattress and walking out.

'It was not me who took the Ledger …' said Lily, trying her best to not let the quiver in her voice show. She was flushed under her collar, red with indignation at being openly humiliated, but she spoke up nonetheless. Very softly at first, and then a bit louder. The video spoke for itself. 'I am sorry to say that it was DJ. But why DJ did this, I don't know...' she said, looking at him, hoping he would offer an explanation. 'I thought he was a friend.'

'And just who do you think you are to ask or question any one of us?' said Lady Devi.

'Hang on a minute, Lady Devi. We need to ask DJ what he was doing there,' said King Khair.

Everyone looked at DJ.

'So, DJ, was it in fact you? Tell me, was it you? It certainly looks a lot like you,' said King Khair.

'Yes ... it was me.'

A loud gasp swept through the ballroom.

'And why, pray, would you do that?' asked King Khair calmly.

'I did it because—' began DJ, with a quiver in his voice.

And before DJ could say anything else at all, Lady Devi interrupted him.

'He did no such thing. This has all clearly been done by the palace intruder, who is nothing but trouble.'

'Let him speak for himself, if you don't mind, Lady Devi,' said King Khair. 'DJ, did you plant the Ledger in Lily's room?'

'Yes, I did,' said DJ, his gaze downcast but his voice crystal clear.

'Does that mean you had the Ledger with you all this time?'

'It wasn't with me, but I knew who had it.'

'You did? So why didn't you speak up instead of planting it in Lily's room? Is there someone you are protecting who had the Ledger?'

'Oh, he is such a good, gullible soul,' said Lady Devi, interrupting again. 'DJ, why are you trying to protect Lily?'

'I wanted to protect the gifts of nature, the mystic boons,' said DJ with some effort, for it was clearly difficult for him to contradict his mother.

'Pfft! These so-called boons, you are all treating them with kid gloves. Fools are they who don't reap the opportunities that lie before them. We could all be so much richer than we are. But no, we do not want to upset the lay of the land. Who cares about these mystic boons! What use are they if not for you and me? Vipin and I would have earned a fortune. And DJ, you would be ruling a powerful, wealthy island.'

'I beg your pardon, what did you say?' said the King.

'Oh, nothing, I meant Pashmina would be ruling a very wealthy island whose every magical gift is there for you to profit from. The Ledger has all you need, the only problem is its code. Some ancient undecipherable mumbo-jumbo isn't going to come between us and what's ours.'

'Hold on a second,' said the King. 'The only person who knows the language of the Ledger is Quill. No one has bothered to ask him what's in the Ledger all these years. Why are you so interested only now?'

To everyone's surprise, DJ spoke up instead.

'When the mall, breeding zoo and every other one of my mum and Vipin's plans were stopped by Quill, who wanted to protect the mystic boons, my mum sensed an opportunity.'

'"Where others see obstacles, I see opportunity." Yes, that's right, Lady Devi's favourite quote,' said Sir Vipin.

DJ went on, 'So, when they realized that the boons were all over the island, they wanted to find out what they were. Quill clearly knew but he never wrote it down.'

'Yes,' said Lady Devi. 'All those years of tinkering in the den should amount to something.'

'So, they took my help to bug his den. Quill doesn't know that he talks to himself. Whenever he makes a scientific discovery, he narrates it out loud to himself … So, bit by bit, he himself was leaking the Ledger, and we had these bits of information that we tried to use.'

'We made sense of his annoying muttering, and let's just say we were surprised at what we learned. Why should all this knowledge stay with one man? It was ours to use too. Finders, keepers,' said Lady Devi.

'So why did you take the Ledger?' asked the King.

'Well, we got sick and tired of waiting for him to solve these boons one at a time! We'd figure it out for ourselves, we thought.'

Sir Vipin looked like he had seen a ghost. Lady Devi had just confessed to stealing the Ledger.

'Oh, she didn't steal it, Sir, just borrowed it, you know, to have a crack at it,' said Sir Vipin.

'Oh yes,' said Lady Devi, turning on the flower in her speech like she did when she wanted to flatter and please. 'Of course not, I merely took it to have a look.'

'I think you can stop talking now, Mum … I think you've said enough,' said DJ wryly. 'I knew you and Vipin would eventually spill the beans. That's why I planted the Ledger—knowing it would be found—and then let you expose yourself.'

Lady Devi flew into a rage. 'Is this your grand ambition? Of being nothing but a patternmaker to that heir-head?'

'I think you have said enough, Lady Devi,' said King Khair. 'I would like to stop you right there. DJ, you need to explain why you put it in Lily's room. Did you know you were going to get caught? You can't have known about the camera.'

'Oh, I knew about the camera alright. It does studio lighting for our photoshoots, it gives you background music, it even tells jokes, Of course, it has a CCTV camera that records every move. I just made sure it was pointing in my direction and could get a clear read of my face.'

They looked at the footage again. DJ walked in with his cap, and they noticed him ever so slightly tilt his face up as he left the room.

'I knew I would get recorded. I also knew that when I confessed, my mother would eventually expose her plans. It was just a matter of time before she got ahead of herself. And I needed her to stop putting the island in danger.'

'You stupid boy, you stupid, stupid boy, what have you done?' yelled Lady Devi.

'He has done nothing except to put an end to your nonsense, which I have been bearing unknowingly all this while,' said the King. 'The question is, what do we do with you?'

'I might have let her give herself away, but in return, I ask you to please treat her kindly, Your Majesty,' said DJ.

'We have always known that the island is protected by its own people, their words and deeds. We do not have a jail, we do not have gallows, so the only thing we can do is banish you, Lady Devi,' said the King gravely. 'As for you, Sir Vipin, you as the Island Minister deserve some recognition for successfully keeping me in the dark, it seems, to one day rule with DJ as the puppet king! You will be tried in our highest court … and banished.'

'Nothing of the sort, Your Majesty. Only when power resides with you, can you decide what you want to do with it,' said Sir Vipin, revealing a whole new visage to the King.

'Guards, take him,' said the King calmly.

But before they could, Sir Vipin opened a casket hidden under his silk scarf. He dramatically brought it out and, like a magician, lifted his sleeve to reveal the rings on his finger. One of the rings was in the shape of a prism. He held it against the sunlight streaking into the glass ballroom. Then, he started to open the small casket to reveal what he had inside it—the Opal!

A horror-stricken gasp went through the room. Everyone froze on the spot. Sir Vipin pointed the prism right onto the

Opal, sending sharp rays of reflected sunlight into its very heart. And as he did that, he laughed loud and hard.

'Now, try *this* in the highest court, Your Majesty. Bagradoo never did deserve its own riches. Who are you to tell us not to

profit from the island's boons? Of what use are they if not for us to rule the island, to hold power in the world?'

The guards seized Sir Vipin as he concluded his speech, all the while shining the prism on the Opal for as long as he could. He only managed six seconds before the Opal was wrested from his hands and he was handcuffed.

But it was too late. The prism ring had only made the sunrays all the more powerful, sending the calm, clear Opal churning to a disturbed cloudy colour. Within moments, as if reflecting the crystal's changing mood, the sky started to turn cloudy, and soon it was as if a grey blanket had been pulled overhead. The sunlit glass ballroom turned gloomy. A carpet of rainclouds covered the sky as if it was there to stay for ever, making a blue sky nothing but a distant dream.

'Oh no,' said Quill, looking up at the sky as a few raindrops started to fall. 'Your Majesty, I'm sorry to say these might just be the first few drops of the beginning of an endless rain.'

'The endless rain,' said King Khair, in a calm and composed voice that only betrayed the smallest tremor.

Lily could tell that he was masking a deep concern, a deep unease that seemed to cloud his face as the sky darkened.

'What is the endless rain, Dad? I thought it was just a myth. I didn't know it could actually happen ...' said Pashmina,

hoping her dad would, as he always did, allay her worst fears. But the King could not. He simply had to speak the truth, no matter how difficult. At a moment like this, there was no use sugar-coating anything.

'Pashmina, here is something I hoped you would never have to see. If this is really an endless rain, it is not in our power to stop it. Usually, the rain stops when the clouds empty themselves, but here the clouds don't empty themselves. They can't. They are endlessly stuck in a storm-like condition that does not cease. Such is the unrest in the sky, created by this curse.'

'Dad, surely you don't believe in curses. You said you did not,' said Pashmina, sounding almost like a child who doesn't like what she is told.

'I don't, Pashmina, of course I don't. Or should I say I never ever wanted to because that would not be a good example to set to my people. But the mystic boons have always had a flip side, and here on the island, any gift when misused has a powerful ability to turn everything on its head. This is what is referred to in the Ledger of Boons as a twisted force.'

'But Dad, you said you did not believe in the twisted forces of the Ledger.'

'I never did want to make a big deal out of the Ledger because I knew that it was ripe for being misused. It is best if people simply don't believe in magic. If they do, those with the wrong plans may try to get it, to misuse it. The safest place for the Ledger was therefore always in bright daylight, unguarded in a messy study where no one bothers to keep anything under lock and key. But now that the twisted force of the Opal has come into play, I have no choice but to declare an emergency.

'Well done, Lady Devi. If there was something more you wanted, you could have just asked me. And Vipin, what a sad example you have been to the future generations who would aspire to hold office in the palace.

'Guards, you may as well take Vipin and Devi away to their respective rooms and keep them under surveillance, though what further damage they can possibly do, I don't know. Deploy our troops to every corner of Bagradoo, to help the people reach higher ground. Tell everyone to get up on their terrace. We will send them food and other supplies. We will transport them out of the island if needed, but no harm will come to my people. I, their King, however, will not leave this island. I will be here come rain or shine, to see this day through.' And with that, the King collapsed into his armchair.

'Oh, Daddy,' said Pashmina, running up to him. She leaned her head on his shoulder to offer him comfort and cry a little at the same time.

'I am sorry, Pashmina. I have let this descend upon you on an occasion that was supposed to be your big day. Look at what you are inheriting ... an endless rain.'

'And a lot of new pets, by the look of it,' said a frail yet determined voice with a distinct tone of humour. It was the Dowager Queen. 'Come on, young man. This is no time to collapse,' she said to her son, the King. 'Khair, my boy, you are the King. What are you going to do to stop this flood?'

'There is nothing I can do, Mother, nothing.'

'Well, we will have to think of something, because I will not live to see my home of sixty years get washed away. We are the Bagradaens, young man, and the Bagradaens do not give up without a fight. Also, if we don't act now, Bagradoo Palace may soon become the world's largest indoor zoo!' She tapped the felt-tipped end of her cane on the glass to signal the view outside. Creatures big and small seemed to be climbing up the fort to get away from the floods in the valley.

'Please, no more crocodiles in my bedroom!' cried Pashmina.

'You will be lucky if there are just crocodiles.'

'Oh, there's Parumm!' said Pashmina and Lily together, melting at once on seeing their favourite baby elephant in the courtyard.

'Oh dear, it looks like we have all lost the plot,' said the Dowager Queen.

Lily was listening to all of this and wondering why Quill had not spoken up yet.

'Quill,' she said softly to him, but everyone turned to hear. 'If the Opal is a gift of nature, and the endless rain a twisted force, there must be a cure, right?'

'It is true,' said Quill. 'It is true, but I have not yet deciphered the code for it. I have tried for years and failed. Please accept my resignation, Sir, please do. I have failed the palace when the palace most needed me. I should have been able to translate the code by now. But the secret language of the ultimate gift of nature was beyond me. I only know so far as to explain that the Opal should be kept away from light.'

'That's all very well, and yours was a good speech,' said the Dowager Queen without much sentimentality. 'But time and tide wait for no one, so let us get to the bottom of this. Who can help Quill?'

'My mom,' said Lily. 'My mom is a scientist and she told me to call her if we needed any help. Is it okay if I tell her what is going on? She usually has some good ideas.'

'Why, yes,' said the Dowager and Quill together.

'Now, come on, my boy, our King—you have been a great ruler and we are all with you. There is no time to brood. You have always loved the water, to you it is a friend. So, consider this a friendly fight with the flood that you must win.'

'Sand!' exclaimed the King suddenly. 'Sand is what we need, heaps of it. We certainly don't have enough right now … We need dunes and dunes of it. And we need an army greater than ours to pack the banks.'

'Strike,' said Pashmina. 'We should ask the thief Strike.'

'Yes, he does have a rather motley crew of islanders always ready to help him. That's why he has remained this slippery for so long.'

'Does that mean he gets a royal pardon?'

'Yes, he does, he gets a royal pardon. In the hour of need, in the hour of flood, at times of crisis, we must forgive where we can … forgive wisely but forgive nonetheless,' said the King, renewed with vigour.

'I've got Mom on the video conference line,' said Lily. 'I'll take her through everything. Mom, I need to catch you up with what's going on … are you ready?'

Lily speed-talked her mother through the issue, to everyone's amazement.

'Speed-talking—an underrated advantage of being a vlogger,' remarked Al the Pal in a robotic voice.

Everyone tried to suppress a laugh so as not to make light of the moment, but it worked and lightened the mood.

'I'm sensing a two per cent reduction in overall stress in the room,' said Al the Pal.

'I think that will be good for now,' said Lily trying to shush him.

Lily's mother listened, and then in true mom-style, she got right to the point.

'Hello everyone, I am Lily's mother, Rita. Thank you for so kindly hosting my daughter. I wish we could have met in a less urgent situation. But here is my reading of things. If these unusual rains continue to fall at the present rate, you will have water at the doorstep of the palace in about six hours. If the sandbags are air-dropped successfully then you can, at best, delay the water for another six hours. With the palace being the highest point on the island, the people of Bagradoo might just have to be up on the rooftops. I suppose the entire human population of the island could fit there with a squeeze. But what about the animals?'

'We need to stop the rain, and I'm afraid that doesn't seem to be in anyone's hands,' said the King. 'We are sending for air ambulances, and they are all on their way. We have friends, neighbours—like the Emperor of Kaftan—and well-wishers around us, not to mention a top-notch island rescue team. The Bagradoo can-do spirit is enshrined in the heart of every Bagradaen. It is time for us to come together.'

As the King went on with his rather emotional speech, Rita interrupted to ask, 'Has this kind of rain occurred before?'

No one said anything for a few moments, until the Dowager Queen spoke.

'Yes, my dear, it has, and it is something only few of us living today can say that they remember. Some of us prefer not to remember. Many moons ago, we had a day of endless rain. A formidable flood followed, when many lives were simply washed away. It did not stop until all was but lost.'

'I don't believe in spells and cures, I'm afraid,' said Rita across the airwaves. 'The only fixes I have at my disposal are all entirely scientific. I have nothing against your trying the time-tested cures you have at hand, but they may be nothing more than wishful thinking.'

'But then there's the Ledger. What about the stuff in it?' said Quill. 'It is a strange mix of science and magic. It is the magic of nature itself and the strange, uncontrolled repercussions of not respecting this magic that I have been studying in great awe and humility all these years.'

Rita listened closely.

'Decades of work has helped me decode some of it but has only got me so far. The Ledger is in a language, a complex system of codes that is very hard to decode. I have worked for years to try and unlock the answers to the eternal rain.'

'I am afraid I can't help you with spells,' said Rita.

'These are not just spells; these are mysteries of nature. It is just that here on the island they work in magical ways and their language is in code to protect them. I have translated hundreds of couplets about the mystic boons, but I can't go beyond this page about the rain.'

'Mom, I have an idea. Can't your algorithm robot help?' asked Lily, suddenly.

'You mean your little computer over here?' asked the Dowager sceptically.

'Well, the computer we sent with Lily is just a small version of the one we have built, that is used to decode hidden patterns.

Perhaps it might work for an ancient language. I can't promise it will work … but we can certainly try,' said Rita.

Quill sat down, cleared his throat and slowly started to read out the translations to the spells he had decoded so far. He showed Rita the script of the strange language and shared the pages with her, muttering all along that never in his wildest dreams did he think that he would share Bagradoo's secrets with someone outside the palace. But here he was doing exactly that at a time of emergency when he simply had to trust Lily's mom.

As Rita put it all into her master robot, the original Al that she had invented, everyone watched. The robot, a giant grey box full of buttons and knobs, beeped and grunted, purred and rattled on the screen like a giant refrigerator meets spacecraft meets printer. Quill showed page after page of the Ledger to the computer, which scanned it remotely and then seemed to eat up the words whole.

It then started to spit out a bunch of paper sheets with code words printed on them. Lily's mother looked at the words and the screen on the computer in wonder. 'A pattern is emerging, enough to translate the language. Does this make sense, Professor Quill?

'When skies rain down in an endless spell,
They stop when they hear the old conch shell,
And with its calming, peaceful sound,
Hope that was lost will now be found.'

'I told you, the Ledger likes a good rhyme,' said Quill, jubilant.

'Okay, people. We have a flood to stop,' said Al the Pal, acting like the true sidekick to the big robot on the screen.

'The conch shell!' said the King. 'The conch shell sits in a case at the highest point in the palace. It has not been sounded for years.'

The King walked up the spiral stairs to the domed tower at the very top of the palace. Quill, Lily, Pashmina, DJ and even the Dowager Queen followed.

Inside was a small glass cupboard with antique heirlooms, turquoise and coral ornaments and the conch shell kept on cushions. Though clearly very important, no one had opened the cupboard in a long time.

The King brought out a bunch of keys and one at a time tried to open the lock. Everyone waited until about ten keys later, they heard a click. The door of the glass case opened. The King paused, took a breath and then picked up the conch shell.

'Sir,' said Quill. 'It needs to sound around the island. Everyone needs to hear it. The sound has to cut through the rumbling skies and create a serene calm that pushes the clouds away.'

'I hope my old lungs are up to the task,' said King Khair. 'Okay, no pressure then.'

He took a deep breath. At first, a little squeak was all he managed. And then, with one more big gulp of air, he sounded the loudest possible calming sound anyone had ever heard. For a loud sound, it really was calm; for a calm sound, it really was quite loud.

All noise and activity came to a standstill. Everyone looked up, even the deer, birds, elephants, squirrels, rhinos and crocs. They all looked up at the glass tower. Everything fell silent except for the rain that kept falling … and the sound of the conch, both now equally loud. It was as if they were in a duel to go on forever. As the King pushed a final gust of air into the conch, it felt like the entire land, sky and water shook for some moments before the conch's sound began to taper slowly but beautifully.

This was the countdown of the conch's power—it would either work, or it would not. Over the next few seconds, the sound trailed off. Everyone had their eyes on the sky. And, just as the last echo of the conch reverberated through the thick air, the rain's last drop fell. *Plop!*

That was it, everyone cheered! Hurrah! It looked like the animals were cheering too, waiting to watch the clouds clear. The first hint of sunrays filtered through the glass tower in a beautiful streak of light.

'I told you, the answers are always right here on the island,' said King Khair. 'With the help of good friends and well-wishers, you can find them.'

As they made their way down, ready to cheer, they saw the Dowager in a pool of tears. The King was quite distraught at this sight of his otherwise very composed mother, the picture of equanimity and poise.

'Mother! Why this new flood? I'm too out of breath for a new gust into the conch shell.'

The Dowager looked up, her eyes still streaming. 'These are tears of joy, my boy, tears of joy. The flood had brought back my worst fears and yet, healed my darkest wounds.'

They heard another snort, which seemed to be coming from the video screen. It was Lily's mother blowing her nose.

'What are we to do if all the calm people start to melt into puddles?' quipped Al. 'We can't afford another flood.'

'She who was lost has now been found. And there is no greater present than finding a true friend of the family. Our little Lily, *our* Lily is no longer Bagradoo's visiting traveller, she is one of us. She came as a tourist and will leave as a cherished friend,' the Dowager said.

Lily's heart melted. Pashmina came to hug Lily. 'I always wanted a partner in crime. So, DJ … we have another one here we can get up to mischief with!'

'How I wish that things could have been easier,' said DJ. 'I feel terrible that Mum caused all this trouble. Well, she is where she belongs, and we are keeping her out of trouble for as long as we can.'

'And now, we have a ball to prepare for!' said the King. 'Pashmina will be crowned the heir on this day of her debutante ball.'

So, with much fanfare, it happened. The Opal was brought out from under its velvet cloak and placed on top of Pashmina's crown, giving her a glow of iridescent light, making her strong to rule the land when her time came.

Then, it was time for Lily to leave. She kissed everyone in fond farewell. 'I promise to be in touch,' she said to Quill,

Pashmina, the King, DJ and the Dowager, who each took turns to give her the warmest goodbye embrace.

'We have found you, and you are ours and we are yours, my dear,' said the Dowager Queen. 'You may have come from afar, but you will always belong to Bagradoo.'

'We know you want to go home to Puddleton, but please know that you belong just as much right here, in Bagradoo,' the King said.

As Lily was sent off in a grand farewell on the cruise ship, she knew she had a lot of vlogging left to do. But she could only share the tiniest sliver of what she had experienced. She couldn't possibly spill the secrets of the Island of Bagradoo.

Back at school on the first day after summer, Sasha walked up to Lily.

'So, Lily,' she said loudly so that everyone could hear her. 'I heard you spent your summer in a palace, huh? Did they treat you like a princess? Does that make you royal?'

'Well, not exactly royal, but royal-ish,' said Al the Pal from her backpack.

Lily laughed.

Sasha looked stunned. 'What was that?'

'Oh, just my talking robot …'

'Still so weird …' muttered Sasha to her friends. But then she turned around and said, 'I hear your Glog's doing pretty well. Wanna feature your gumboots on the Shlog?'

'I'll check her calendar and get back to you,' said Al.

Lily tried hard not to laugh as Sasha looked affronted. 'Sure, why not, Sasha,' she said. 'I'd love that.'

Epilogue

Eight Months Later

Lily is in her room, blogging about her latest find in the local pond to what is now her sizeable fashion and nature fan following around the world.

She gets a ping on Al the Pal:

'Lily … a few strange things have been happening here in Bagradoo. Any chance of coming down for another visit?

—Love, Pash.'

About the Author

Amrita Gandhi is a television host, writer and producer who studied anthropology in England as an undergraduate and postgraduate student. She had the chance to visit and stay as a palace guest at known and less-known palaces around India when she hosted a royal-themed travel show for NDTV Goodtimes.

Amrita recently moved to California with her husband and their two daughters. In her spare time, she pursues her love for acting and singing.

About the Illustrator

Lee-Roy Lahey is a cartoonist, illustrator and storyboard artist. He has worked for over twenty years in film and television, for animation studios such as Nickelodeon and Disney and on the Oscar-nominated feature 'Anomalisa'. Lee-Roy's art also appears in *The Loud House* (Papercutz) and *Monster Elementary* (Space Goat/Broken Oar).

He lives in Los Angeles, California, with his wife, two daughters, one cat and a really rather modest collection of Pez dispensers, no matter what his wife says.